COOKING FOR AN ENGLISHMAN

A novel by Alex Adon

With recipes devised by Caroline Krantz

Published by Alex Adon

Copyright 2016 Alex Adon

With special thanks to Sara Jolly

A Meal With One Olive
Moussaka The Greek Way
Coffee Cake
Pickled Cucumbers
Pomegranate Ices
Flying Sardines
Cold Dogs
Washed Lamb And Lentils
Semolina Soup (Lost Recipe)
Different Dumplings
Banana Fritters With Raspberry Sauce
Turkish Coffee
Rahat Lokum Turkish Delight
Eggs Voilà!
Balls Of Fire
Heavenly Flapjacks
Pickled Herring With Salad
Mrs Wildblood's Sandwiches
The Treasure's Pasties
Restorative Soup
Wild Strawberry Pancakes
Cider Apple Pork
Sweetbreads À La André
Sweetest Shish Kebabs
Jumping Jack Rarebit
Sisters Pudding
Not Napoleon's Fish
Utah's Cauliflower
Paw Paw
Ahmed's Skewers
A Cake Of Fruit
Hindi Tea
Muscovy Duck Casserole
Perfect English Pork Chop

A MEAL WITH ONE OLIVE

Rustic Bread sliced thickly
Olive oil
Thyme
Garlic
Salt and Pepper
A black olive

Dab the slices liberally with oil, rub with a cut clove of garlic, and sprinkle with thyme and seasonings, warm in the sun or in an oven for a few minutes to amalgamate the flavours. Enjoy with a black olive.

The father found a dark conical tree thrusting through rocks and sand to shade the children. There they waited in the heat for him to finish his work. Afterwards, he had promised, there would be lovely food for them all.

The girl who was about seven, had been put in charge of the smallest child, a pale eyed copper headed toddler they called Pup, with instructions to keep him out of the sun. She wore a faded polka dot yellow cap-sleeved dress and sandals. Her hair, dark, coarse, was gripped to one side with an enamel slide depicting a sprig of edelweiss. She was called Leila. It meant dark as night, her mother once told her.

'You came out of me in a night without moon or stars. Like your eyes. Like your hair. Black. Everything was black.'

'The talk of the mad,' her father said. Leila was his grandmother's name.

The mother's name was Sabina. A name you give a dog, his people said. The children's father had many names. Mr Adon, 'Adoni', it meant a God. The children's mother who was a blonde from Europe called him Johnny. Her family called him Johannes but his family called him Youssef. He now called himself Joe.

' "Joe" is international. It means no one can tell from where you come or to where you go. They can put nothing on you.' This he learnt in prison where he was put for selling passports.

'Give them nothing, no information. If they say the sun is yellow you say it is green. Give them nothing, nothing to use against you.' He would laugh and scream in his sleep, words and sounds that were not connected.

The boy, called Ben, a year or so older than Leila but shorter and slighter, wearing shorts and a thin cotton shirt, was drawing an object in the sand with a piece of wire. Leila peered at the drawing.

'Is it an insect?' she asked.

'It's a machine gun.'

Using her forefinger she began making her own picture in the sand.

'What's that supposed to be?' Ben asked.

'Fruit.'

'Fruit!'

'That's an orange, that's a banana, that's another orange...'

'Oranges aren't round.'

'Yes they are!'

'Not properly round.' Ben scuffed the gun with his foot back into sand and walked towards the road. Vehicles shot past blowing dust upwards.

In the culvert on the opposite side of the road the children's father worked with a pickaxe. His cream jacket hung like a headless scarecrow on a stick beside a mound of stones.

Ben called: 'How long are you going to be?'

'Don't cross the road,' Mr Adon shouted. 'Stay till I finish.'

His narrow shoulders propped up an aristocratically long neck and a head once considered handsome. City bred, not built for manual work, he looked exhausted. He had fallen on unlucky times.

On his first day out of jail he sought his children and found them in a dead village close to the prison abandoned into the care of an aged woman who screeched at him for money owed. The children's limbs were sore with fleabites and the girl's hair sticky with lice. He thrust a fist of notes into the old woman's bandaged hand and pushed her away as she wailed for more.

'Come with me', he bade the children. 'Come!' They ran with him from the top floor of the ancient building down wide worn stone steps into the streets.

The old woman kept up the screeching until they were out of sight. When she had opened her hand there was only one note. The rest was cut up Bible paper.

They walked along the road out of town until they came to a petrol station. Their father led the children to the yard at the back where broken vehicles were parked and told them to wait. He returned with a tin cup from which he dabbed their hair with petrol and then washed it out with water from the hose.

He promised them food. Soon. Only first they must find a place to stay. Smelling of petrol, their clothes still wet they followed him to the forecourt.

'Be patient. Be good children.'

He suddenly left them to chase after a passing bread vendor on a three-wheeler. He returned with a large round of flat soft warm bread. He handed the bread to Leila.

'Wait,' he said. 'Wait here till I come.'

The children could see him in the garage cafe across the way drinking from a small glass. He came out with his head down, his hands in his pockets.

'Look,' he said, opening his hand. 'Look what I brought for you.' In his palm were four crinkled dull black olives. The children and their father sat on the ground where he showed them how to make a meal with one olive and a slab of bread.

First you suck the olive to make spit and oil your throat. Then you take it out and you bite the smallest bite from the top of the olive, small small, small. Your mouth is now ready for the bread.

Now the bread tastes good and can go down easy. And now you do it again and if you are very clever and skilled at the end you have finished the bread and are satisfied and you still have the stone of the olive to suck and keep your mouth moist.

A woman wearing sunglasses and a silk beige scarf over her hair watched them as her car was filled with fuel. She wore a trouser suit the same colour as the scarf. She was rich. Everything about her - the creamy skin, the coral lipstick, the pale high-heeled shoes, the shine on her new car told she was rich.

In a quiet voice she instructed the petrol boy to check the tyres and sauntered over to the children and their father. She was French. She talked to Mr Adon with sounds that were aloof, a serious face, scowling a little as she tilted her head looking at him this way and that as she talked, at odds with the playful challenging movements of her hands and shoulders.

Even though Leila could not understand what the woman was saying or what the word was for it she knew the woman was flirting with her father. She glared at the woman as she watched her father in his stained linen suit straighten himself and pat down his hair. Ben was more interested in the woman's car.

'This lady enquires,' Mr Adon addressed the children, 'would we like a lift in her car.'

Ben tugged at his father's sleeve. 'Say yes!'

Leila said: 'No. We don't want to.'

The woman laughed and returned to wait in her car.

'Oh come on,' her father attempted to cajole Leila. 'We have nowhere else to go.'

Leila shook her head. 'I'm not going to, I'm not going to,' she said over and over again looking at the ground. Ben kicked her and she kicked him back. Their father bade them stop and went over to the woman and they spoke a few moments, shook hands and then she drove away.

Mr Adon carried Pup but did not speak to Leila for a long time. It was dusk and they still had a long way to walk before reaching the place where they would sleep for the night. Mr Adon walked so quickly the children had to scurry to keep up with him. 'Your fault,' Ben hissed to his sister. 'We could be in her car.' She nudged him away and said nothing. Her legs were tired and her head tender and itching from the petrol. She felt in disgrace.

'We wouldn't be walking if it wasn't for you!' her brother continued to berate Leila.

'I didn't like her!' She didn't like the way the woman had made her feel ugly. She didn't like the way she had made her father try to pretend what he wasn't any more. She didn't like the woman's powdery smell.

'She said we could go in her car!'

'Enough. Leave your sister alone.'

'I didn't like her,' Leila repeated. 'I didn't want to be in her car.'

'She always spoils things,' Ben kicked Leila again.

'She gave us somewhere to stay anyway,' their father said 'for some work.'

The sun was setting when they reached the orange grove. An old man in a cracked leather jacket was waiting for them. They followed him single file along the irrigation troughs and a smell of rotting fruit to a cement hut. Outside there was a standpipe and a stack of boxes. Inside there was a light switch and a primus stove, a bunk bed and some cups and pans. Broken rusted wire mesh had been crushed into the window opening. The old man switched on the light and bade them goodnight.

'Look,' the children's father smiled, 'she has left something for us.'

In a wooden food safe hanging on wire from the ceiling was a packet of ground coffee, a jar of olives and a loaf of bread.

'Now we will have a feast.'

They stayed in the hut for three days eating oranges and eking out the olives and bread. On the second day the woman came in her car to watch the children's father work. He could stay and earn money, maybe do easier work but the children would need to be taken into a home. She could arrange it for him. Come to the house when you have decided, the woman said.

Mr Adon visited the woman in her house and returned early the next morning smelling of the woman's powder. He told the children to wash. They were leaving. He had money in his wallet again. The few remaining olives and bread they left behind.

MOUSSAKA THE GREEK WAY

1 kilo (2 lbs) aubergines, sliced
Some good olive oil
500 g (1 lb) minced lamb
1 big onion, chopped
4 cloves garlic, finely chopped
2 - 3 ripe tomatoes or 2 tablespoons tomato puree
2 teaspoons oregano
2 teaspoons cinnamon
A bunch of flat-leafed parsley, finely chopped
500 ml (1 pint) full cream milk
60 g (2 oz) butter
4 level tablespoons plain flour
Fresh nutmeg
Grated Graviera cheese (or gruyere)
Salt
Pepper

Sprinkle the aubergines with salt and leave for about an hour until they are covered with little black drops (this is the bitterness). Wash and dry them thoroughly, brush them with oil and grill them on both sides until they just begin to become soft.

Fry the onions in 3 tablespoons of olive oil until soft and golden, add the garlic and fry until you smell the aroma. Add the meat, lower the heat and cook until it changes colour, stirring to break up the lumps. Add the oregano, cinnamon, tomato, salt and lots of black pepper cover the pan and cook on a low heat until the sauce becomes thicker. If it is very oily remove some of the oil and then add the flat-leafed parsley.

For the béchamel sauce, heat the milk then remove from heat. Melt the butter over a very low heat. Let it cool a little then sprinkle in the flour and whisk it until it is smooth. Turn the heat on again and heat *slowly for 1 - 2 minutes, stirring occasionally. Add the milk a few tablespoons at a time whisking the mixture until it is smooth before adding more. Continue until all the milk has been added. Keep cooking and stirring until the sauce thickens. Season with salt, pepper and grated nutmeg.*

Assemble the moussaka in a baking dish. Arrange the aubergines, cover with the meat filling and finish by adding the béchamel sauce. Sprinkle with cheese and nutmeg and bake for 30- 45 minutes at 350F /180C/ Gas mark 4.

Mr Adon was a wonderful storyteller. The stories he told in the shaky big iron bed he shared with the children stretched into the dark until they slept. This was the golden period of the father's stories, the ones they remembered into adulthood.

Each night, supporting the boys in one arm, Leila in the other, he laid his head back against the iron rails of the bed and with his eyes searching the flaking blue tinged whitewashed ceiling, he'd begin.

He gave out the stories like pieces of special cake, making the children hungry for them with the promise: 'What I am telling you now you will never find in a book. What I am telling you, I swear by God, is true. It happened to me.'

The children would beg him to begin. 'Start it,' they pleaded. 'Start the story.' There were times when the children were unable to follow the stories completely. However, they always found something to enjoy since their father had a talent for special effects.

When people kissed in his stories he kissed the children, when they shouted, he'd shout, when they cried he would cry too. When characters in his stories ran he moved his legs up and down in the bed and when they died he was scary. He groaned, rolled his eyes wildly, prayed and wailed before coughing into a dying choke. And then he'd lie motionless for a long time. No pleas to wake up, tickling, pulling his hair, would make him move.

Once he was so carried away in a death scene, the children panicked. They jumped out of the bed and hit him with a broom. Still he did not move. They threw water on him and he let them do it without a movement. The boy ran to fetch help. A cousin and his wife came and the father let them fuss and wail and make private remarks about him before he sat up and startled the wife into a screaming fit. And then he laughed. And the children laughed and they all went on laughing as the wife left the room sobbing. The cousin stayed and made coffee.

The children's father was still laughing with his hand over his mouth, trying to stop the laughter and blurting out, 'Excuse me.... excuse me...'. After a while he stopped to drink the coffee and the children returned to the bed to listen to their father and the cousin talk of the restaurant business and politics. And now instead of laughing he was crying and rocking on the bed.

The cousin made more coffee and lit cigarettes for them both and said for the children's sake he should stop crying now. It was enough. The woman was rubbish and good riddance and look, now the children were also crying, so be a man. This made the father very angry and he shouted at the cousin to get out because he was sick of the sight of him.

After the cousin left, and perhaps to make up for making the children cry, the children's father became cheerful and began the bedtime story.

'I was without one coin like a starving dog. I pass a very expensive restaurant where all the important people like to be seen eating. In this restaurant they have one hundred and one dishes on the menu; you can eat anything you like.

When you are very hungry you dream of food. I had been dreaming of Moussaka with the cheese and meat from sheep with soft aubergines with big tomato and wild herbs from the mountains. Only the Greeks know how to make it. One day you will taste it. It is lovely. But how to get it when you have no money?

Your father, sometimes, he can be a very clever man. You want to know how I get Moussaka without money? I am standing by the restaurant. Moussaka is the speciality of the day, I am dreaming of it, creamy, fragrant Moussaka. Suddenly I see this merchant approach. He looks rich, fat. He is walking, going somewhere, I don't know where. Maybe he has a woman, who knows.

'So you found me', I say to this man who I have never before seen in my life. 'So Okay, I am a man of honour. I pay my debt.' I put my hand on him like he is a brother. 'So tonight I give you full hospitality. We eat at my expense. If you refuse me you insult my name.'

This man he looks at my face, he is amazed. He is puzzled. He does not know how to think about me. I am telling him I owe him something. He is a greedy. A fat man has inside him a hunger which will never be satisfied. He is wanting always one more helping.

So while he is thinking who is this man who will give him a meal for nothing, I am leading him into the restaurant and making important noise with the waiters. I want the very best table, the best menu. The waiters dance round me like I was the Queen of Sheba. The fat man he is very quiet, but he is impressed. So go to sleep now, tomorrow I tell you more.'

Pup was already asleep. The other two were drowsing.

'Tomorrow I must find my way and do my business. You must clean the room a little and wait. In the evening I come back and make a lovely soup with lentils.'

He lit another cigarette. Ben had closed his eyes but Leila clung to her father.

'Finish the story,' she begged. Perhaps she had a premonition it would be the last for a while. She leant her head on his thin chest and could hear his heartbeats.

'Did you eat Moussaka?'

'Tell us the ending,' Ben was awake again.

Mr Adon's cigarette packet was empty. He lit the stub of a cigarette the cousin had left in the brass ashtray.

'Okay, I finish the story. It is nearly finished anyhow.' He held the children closely.

'This fat man he is eating like a starving man. Avocado, fish, soup, meat, everything they have he must taste. Of course I eat very nicely too. Only the best. I beg the fat man, 'Eat a little more my friend, sweets, pastries, cakes, ices'. He is in a paradise. I am forcing him to be what he is: a female pig.

Anyhow he eats and he eats and he drinks, how he drinks. And he is a very happy man. I have made him so happy. He thinks your father is going to pay for his greed. I am telling him all the time he is right to insist I pay my debt to him in full. 'Eat more. Whatever you like. Right is right.'

The time comes to finish the meal. 'Excuse me, my friend', I say. I am holding my stomach. 'I must go to the back to relieve myself'. I leave him with a few little cakes. How do I pay? I don't pay nothing. I whisper to the waiter 'My friend is a rich man and is sending me to bring him a woman' and beg him to chill a little more wine. Then I walk out. My stomach is full and I am free. The fat man, he never see your father again. It is a lovely story, eh? Of course it is true. For a few hours I have made the man happy, for this he must pay. Now you sleep, the story is finished.'

COFFEE CAKE

Oil for greasing
200 ml (⅓ pint) strong black coffee
2 tablespoons cocoa powder
200 g (8 oz) caster sugar
85 g (3 ½ oz) softened butter
½ teaspoon vanilla essence
2 eggs
140 g (6 oz) plain flour
½ teaspoon bicarbonate of soda
1 teaspoon baking powder
1 teaspoon ground cardamom

Preheat oven to 400F/ 200C/ Gas mark 6. Grease a 20 cm cake tin and line the base with greased greaseproof paper. Dust it lightly with sugar and flour. In a saucepan mix the coffee, cocoa and half the sugar and bring to the boil. Simmer for ten minutes and then cool.

Cream the remaining sugar and butter until light and fluffy and add the vanilla essence. Add the eggs and beat into the mixture. If necessary add a little flour to stop the mixture from curdling.

Sift the flour with the bicarbonate of soda, baking powder and cardamom and combine with the butter mixture. Fold in the coffee until the mixture is smooth.

Pour into the cake tin and bake in the centre of the oven for 20 minutes. Turn the temperature down to Gas mark 4 and bake for another 15 minutes or until the sides have shrunk away from the side *of the tin and the top springs back when touched. Remove from the oven and cool, then turn out and dust with icing sugar.*

The children arrived at the aunt's house by bus. She was called Aunt Trudie and was their mother's eldest sister. She was not there to meet them as had been promised but Leila remembered the tall building where the aunt lived and they found it just before dark.

When Aunt Trudie opened the door to see the children standing on the stairs dirty and tired she called her husband. 'Come, come and see what has arrived.' Her short blonde hair was tied back with a white silk scarf and from her ear lobes hung glass earrings in the shape of tears.

The aunt instructed her husband to lay a path of newspapers to the kitchen. The children padded through on dirty feet. While the aunt shouted into the telephone in another room the uncle sat the children on chairs and whispered.

'Do you perhaps like coffee cake?'

He brought the cake down from a cream coloured tin banded with green and lifted from it a fluted moulded pale speckled cake dusted with powdered sugar. His bald head shone as he bent over and carefully cut three thick wedges of the cake.

'Coffee cake,' the uncle announced, his weak grey eyes watering, 'the best you will ever in your life taste. She made it with her own hands.'

He placed each slice on a green glass saucer and then brought orange juice from a jug in the refrigerator. Slices of fresh orange bobbed in the jug. He held them down with a silver spoon to pour the juice into three green tumblers.

'The best orange juice you will ever taste in your life,' he declared. 'I made it myself.'

He stood arms akimbo and waited for the children's reaction. Leila looked at Ben for a signal before she took a small sip of the cold juice. It was a wonderfully sweet and deep sensation. She held the glass to Pup's mouth.

'It's good?' the uncle asked, his large face beaming displaying three gold teeth.

'It's lovely isn't it' Leila addressed Pup by way of response. 'Lovely and orangey. And now we're going to have some cake as well, aren't we?'

It was the mocking mimic adult voice she used in her mother role with Pup. The uncle watched Ben shoot her a scathing glance. Ben had taken a stoical small sip of the juice and carefully placed the glass down again.

'You don't like our cake?' the uncle asked Ben. Leila was already biting into hers.

'It's lovely,' she said wiping crumbs from her lips. 'Lovely and tasty, isn't it,' she addressed Pup again.

Ben threw her of his 'just shut up!' looks. The aunt arrived in the kitchen.

'He doesn't like your cake,' the uncle declared.

'It's very nice,' Ben said biting into it.

Aunt Trudie was in a temper. She tipped the cake into the tin, banged the lid shut with her hand and in German told the uncle to come to the hall.

The children continued to eat the cake. Pup didn't want his.

'Shall I eat it?' Leila asked her brother.

'If you want it.'

'It's good orange juice isn't it?'

'They are not going to keep us', Ben had picked up fragments of the aunt's telephone conversation.

Aunt Trudie's bathroom had cream and green tiles and silver taps. Her bathrobe and shower hat hung like a dead man on a hook on the door. The uncle ran warm water into the bath and laid old towels on the floor.

'Get undressed,' Aunt Trudie ordered. Leila folded her arms and scowled.

'She's shy,' the uncle said. 'Let her wash herself afterwards.'

'What nonsense,' Aunt Trudie's voice rose above the sound of the running water.

'Of what is she shy? Undress,' she instructed again 'and don't be such a stupid child.'

Leila squinted at her aunt's earrings as if she had not heard. She could make them go pink and then mauve with a blink. The uncle turned to Ben and addressed him man-to-man.

'We will leave you to bathe your little brother and then you and your sister can make your own arrangements.'

'This is not a hotel,' Aunt Trudie turned on him. 'We don't supply endless water.'

'Leave them alone,' the uncle said as he led her out. 'Don't make trouble. They are only children.'

'Not my children,' she said, 'not your children.'

Leila washed Pup and then dried him on the floor with her back to the bath while Ben slipped out of his clothes and stepped into the water for a quick dip.

'I'm finished,' he had tied a towel round him. He dried his feet for a long time with his back to her so Leila could wash herself without being looked at. There was a delicacy between them, an unspoken knowledge of things not spoken about, not to be spoken about.

'I didn't really like the cake,' Leila said when they were at the coach station. 'It was too dry.'

They opened the shopping bag their aunt had given them for their onward journey and almost immediately the coach set off. It contained a tube of fruit pastilles, three oranges, beetroot sandwiches, warm orange juice in a screw top marmalade jar which was already leaking and three thin slices of stale coffee cake

PICKLED CUCUMBERS

Enough for two 2 pint jars

2 large good cucumbers
2 tablespoons acetic acid
2 level tablespoons salt
1 level tablespoon sugar
4 level teaspoons mixed pickling spice
4 chillies
2 level teaspoons black peppercorns
2 cloves garlic peeled and chopped

Cut the cucumbers in half lengthways and widthways and then cut into four pieces lengthways. Arrange in the two jars. Put the acid, salt and sugar in a 2 pint measure and fill to the top with cold water. Stir and tip the liquid into the two jars. Add the other ingredients and screw lids on tight. Keep in fridge for four days turning the jars each day. They are now ready to eat.

The German grandmother put them to sleep on soft garden cushions in the spare room at the rear of the house. Leila woke in the night troubled by the strong smell of sourness. She bent over Pup to see if this was where the stench was coming from. He was dry and sweet smelling from the abrasive flannel wash and powdering the grandmother had given them on their arrival.

 'Too late for food now,' she had said.

'It will give you stomach ache.' She made warm milky cocoa in a speckled enamel saucepan and poured it into an assortment of chipped and cracked cups.

She clothed each child in one of her old vests and led them to the back room. 'You stay in this room until I come in the morning.' She patted and kissed each on the head. 'Guten nacht children,' she said. 'No talking,' and switched off the light as she went.

They woke early. The morning light revealed a cement floored room containing several large brown glazed jars. Bunches of herbs and dried flowers hung on nails driven into the masonry. There were tins of oil and rocks of chalk for whitewash in sacks. It was obviously some kind of store.

The room looked out on to a garden of vegetables and fruit trees. Mint and senile geraniums planted in a diverse collection of garden pots and rusting tin cans blocked the path. Beyond were parched fields. Leila visited the toilet adjoining the store and returned to report the grandmother was still asleep. She had peeped into the kitchen. Cups on the table were turned facedown onto plates. The blinds in the sitting room were still down and there was no sound from grandmother's bedroom.

They drank water in cupped hands from the basin in the bathroom. The sun glared into their room. 'I'm hungry,' Leila said to Ben. 'Aren't you?' They listened for the grandmother's footsteps and for noises from the kitchen.

'Go and look again,' Ben commanded.

'You go,' Leila said.

After a while Ben slipped out of the room to find out if grandmother was awake. He returned to report she was still asleep.

'Shall we get some bread from the kitchen?' Leila asked.

'You can.'

Leila didn't want to.

Ben lifted the lid from one of the ceramic jars. Floating in a scum of white alum were dill cucumbers. This was the cause of the sour smell in the room.

Leila loved pickled cucumbers. 'Get me one,' she pleaded. Ben dipped his hand into the pickle jar and pulled out a small ridged cucumber accrued with spices and herbs. Pup didn't like the taste and cried for biscuits.

'Shush,' said Leila, 'you'll wake grandmother.' She and Ben ate four cucumbers each before they heard noises beyond the room. Grandmother was awake. They hurried into the bathroom and washed their hands and mouths to get rid of the smell.

Grandmother had made them hot semolina for breakfast with a dab of red jam in the middle. In between spooning it into Pup's hungry mouth she watched Ben and Leila struggling to eat theirs.

'What is the matter?' she asked.

'I feel sick,' Ben said. 'So do I,' Leila ran out after him to the toilet. They locked the door behind them and would not let the grandmother in before they had completely flushed away the evidence.

POMEGRANATE ICES

This recipe uses the ingredients of the cocktail Tequila Sunrise.

Serves 4

1 pint water
110 g (4 oz) caster sugar
Thinly pared zest and juice of one orange
2 teaspoons lemon juice
3 pomegranates
2 tablespoons tequila

Heat the sugar and water in a heavy based saucepan until the sugar has dissolved. Add the orange zest and boil for 5 minutes until the syrup is tacky. Remove from heat. Cool and strain.

Halve the pomegranates; remove the seeds and juice with a teaspoon. Make sure there is no pith. Stir seeds and juice into the syrup with the tequila and orange and lemon juice.

Pour into an ice tray and freeze. Ten minutes before serving remove from the freezer and break up the granita.

One day the children's mother arrived for a surprise visit. The grandmother had spent the morning making a yeast cake for the occasion. 'It will have all the things she likes', she told the children. 'Marzipan and bitter chocolate and most important, almonds. Your mother loves nuts.' But the ingredients were wasted. After an hour in the bowl placed under a cloth on the cement well top it had not risen at all. 'The yeast must have been dead, maybe I killed it,' the grandmother guessed.

'Maybe too much heat,' she was agitated by the loss of the chocolate and nuts, the eggs and butter she had carefully measured out.

'Your mother will have to eat biscuits. Never mind.'

The grandmother counted twelve biscuits - 'two for all and two for luck' - from a packet and arranged them like a daisy on a glass plate. She strained steeped camomile flowers into a glass jug and added chipped ice. She brushed Leila's hair and tied a mauve ribbon into it to match the dirndl skirt with pockets she had stitched for her. She dressed Pup in a clean romper suit and gave Ben new shorts from the shop to put on for the day.

'Are we going away?' Leila asked.

'Any moment now,' grandmother said, 'your mummy will be here and then we will see what we will do.'

Two buses passed the house and did not stop. Late in the afternoon the grandmother gave the children the biscuits to eat and told them to change out of their best clothes.

'Mummy will come another day,' she reported at bed time.

'There are some dogs who make pups but they don't know how to clean them, how to teach them. All they know is how to breed. She is like that,' Leila had heard her dark aunt Amina say. She had shouted it to a neighbour on another level as she whitewashed the roof top garden when the children had stayed there. Leila had glared at her and Aunt Amina laughed. 'It is the truth darling, you don't like to hear the truth?'

That night Leila had wet the bed again and in the morning Aunt Amina said. 'I've had enough. Your mother's sister she can take her turn.'

In the night the children were woken by the sound of a motor horn and car doors slamming. The outside light came on suddenly and lit a portion of the ceiling in their room. Voices entered the house.

'It's mummy. She's come.'

'Go and see,' Ben instructed.

'You.'

They were still wearing grandmother's vests to sleep in.

'Later,' Ben said. 'I'll do it later.'

The voices from the kitchen became loud and angry. A door banged and shook the house. Then there was only crying and unending sobs.

When the house was quiet and dark and the others were asleep Ben slipped out of the room and searched for his mother. On the kitchen table were three pink and gold pomegranates. In the sitting room there was a pale leather suitcase with metal corners.

Ben crouched outside grandmother's room trying to hear if there was more than one person breathing. Eventually he placed his hands on the fat round door handle and turned it very slowly and pushed it open just a little. On the high carved bed grandmother and his mother lay covered with an embroidered blanket with their backs to each other. Both were fast asleep.

The children's mother came into their room before they woke. Her hair was short and clung to her head like a hat. She wore white high heeled sandals and a blue dress printed with a pattern of sailing boats. 'My darlings,' she said, 'my little darlings.' She sat on the floor and began to cry. The children drew near and she touched them briefly but seemed unable to hold them. Pup sat on the floor by her and pulled at the buttons on her dress. Ben and Leila stood above their mother and waited for her to stop crying.

After a while Ben pulled a handkerchief from his pocket and held it out to his mother. She seemed unable to use it. Leila took it from him and wiped her mother's cheeks and nose. Grandmother came into the room and said mummy was not well today. She must lie down and rest.

After breakfast a taxi came and grandmother helped the children's mother into it.

'Is she going away again?' asked Ben.

'When is she coming back?' Leila asked.

'When she is better,' grandmother said. 'We will know everything.'

After the taxi had gone grandmother announced they would now make ices with the pomegranates their mother had bought for them. They were no good for anything else.

FLYING SARDINES

Baked Butterflied Sardines

12 smallish sardines
Handful of chopped dill
Handful of chopped parsley
Handful of chopped chives
1 small red chilli finely chopped
Juice of half a lemon
2 tablespoons of olive oil
1 clove of garlic, chopped
25 g (10 oz) pine nuts
Salt and freshly ground black pepper
Half a cup of breadcrumbs

To butterfly the sardines

With a pair of kitchen scissors remove the fins and the heads. Cut along from the belly down to the tail and pull out the insides. Open out each fish and place it belly side down. Using your thumb, loosen the backbone and carefully pull it out, snipping it off at the tail end but leaving the two fillets attached by the upper skin. Remove any small bones that are left with tweezers. Wash and dry the fish.

Combine the herbs, garlic, pine nuts and chilli together with a tablespoon olive oil. Mix with breadcrumbs, salt, pepper and lemon juice.

Grease a baking tray with olive oil and lay down the sardines skin side down on the tray. Spread a little of the mixture on each. Drizzle a little olive oil on top. Bake for 8 - 10 minutes until golden.

The next taxi that came to the house brought the German aunt Trudie and her husband who carried a briefcase and a cake tin. The taxi driver followed with two suitcases in each hand and a smaller one under his arm while the aunt nursed a bouquet of flowers in yellow paper. When the taxi arrived the children were some distance away in their tree house.

They had acquired and found many good things for the tree house - dusty cushions, grain sacks, torn faded maroon linen curtains, a rope, a broken chair, a shattered step ladder, a frayed oriental rug and an ornately knotted rope hammock which grandmother said they could use but to be careful. 'We don't want any more sick people in this family.'

Pup was lying in the hammock sucking his thumb when the taxi arrived.

'It's the Germans,' Ben alerted his crew of two. For the past few days the tree house had by agreement become an ocean- going sailing ship. Ben was the navigator climbing into the top branches with a telescope made from rolled cardboard into which a water tumbler had been inserted, on the look-out for pirates and abductors. Leila's task was to eke out and apportion the water and food on their odyssey to find their parents.

Pieces of bread were hardened in the sun and puckered with fragments of orange peel to become ships biscuits contaminated with worms. Pup, dying in the ship's hospital galley, was fed medicines made up by pushing mint leaves into bottles, adding sugar and water and salt and sometimes pepper, and once a bright nasturtium flower poked in with a pencil, shaken and administered from an ivory spoon with a carved elephant head found at the bottom of grandmother's sewing box.

'You will die,' Leila warned Pup 'if you don't swallow the medicine. Blood and snot will come out of your ears and your pee will turn black.'

Every afternoon the children played in their tree house until supper time when the grandmother called them to come in. She would stand at the back of the house facing the fields and clap her hands before calling 'Children, children, come in now...come in now' in a Teutonic voice which in maidenhood had sung Mahler at the family piano.

Today the sun was already drowning into black when the grandmother, followed by the Germans, came out of the house and called them to come in. They were to fly in an aeroplane. Not many children have such a chance. To go up into the sky, up, higher than birds. Imagine. They would cross many seas and lands and arrive in another country where it would be cold which is why they must dress warm with socks and jumpers and crocheted bobble hats.

'Where are we going to in the aeroplane?' Ben asked.

'Your father and mother will meet you,' Aunt Trudie assured them. You will all have new starts in life.'

'Are we going to America?' Leila had heard that if you were lucky you went to America.

'Your granny has bought you tickets. From her savings.'

'You are going to England,' the uncle said. 'I have never been there so I can tell you nothing except they have kings and queens and live in dirty houses.'

The aunt shushed him in German.

'He doesn't mean it,' she told the children. 'The English are normal nice people. Like everybody else in the world you get good and you get bad.' The grandmother said enough talking; the children must have their supper and their bath now because tomorrow will be a long day.

Early next morning the children were woken by the grandmother. As she dressed them in new clothes for their journey they heard a car arrive and beep. 'It's the taxi,' she said 'to take you to the airport.'

The aunt and uncle were already up and urging the grandmother and children to hurry please. 'Aeroplanes don't wait for children,' Aunt Trudie said when Leila wanted to search for her hair slide.

The grandmother gave Leila a packet of biscuits for everybody. Uncle, she said, had a big flask of iced tea for the journey. Ben was to carry the suitcase with the children's clothes and Leila a rucksack with some 'little things' for the departure.

'I will never see you again,' the grandmother said as she kissed them in the garden. Her eyes were like moist sultanas. She was crying without sounds. 'Tell your mother to write me a line, if she can find time.'

Aunt Trudie again said, 'We will be late.' The grandmother nodded, she had heard but she had not finished.

To Leila she said: 'Send me a nice postcard of London with your kisses.'

To Ben she said: 'Take care of the others. You are the eldest. Don't be like your father.'

She said 'Grow good,' to Pup and kissed them all again before standing upright. 'Safe journey, and many kisses to your mummy,' were her last words.

The hostess on the aeroplane wore a navy blue lapelled suit and open necked white blouse and was called Jeanette. She was tall with tightly drawn back brown hair and orange lipstick and smelt of crushed flowers. She smiled at everyone and told the children they could sit at the back close to her and the toilets.

The plane was small and tightly packed. After it was airborne Ben went for a walk in it. There were people asleep with their mouths open, some were reading. A woman smiled at him and a man said something to him in a language that was a bit but not exactly like Arabic. Ben did not understand but nodded as if he did.

Pup slid off his seat and crawled into the gangway from where he made fast progress towards the front of the plane and only stopped when he banged his head and cried. Leila went to retrieve him.

'I don't want you lot running up and down my plane,' Jeanette said.

'If you need anything stand on the seat and press this button and if you feel sick use the paper bags. Now be good. There are prizes for well behaved children,' she winked at a passenger on route to the toilets. Intermittently she lobbed them small surprises: sweets, paper and pencils, cards and a pair of dice.

The children tried to blow the sick bags into balloons to make noise bombs but the bags were too sturdy.

'Lunch,' Jeanette announced handing them each a covered tray.

'It smells fishy,' Leila said cautiously peeling back the cardboard cover. 'Fishy and eggy.'

'Flying fish,' Jeanette said

'Open wide,' she said to Pup. 'Frogs and snails for you.' The toddler's lunch was mashed banana mixed with orange juice. 'Open wide,' she repeated. Pup lapped the banana mixture from the spoon Jeanette held out to him. He gurgled and smiled at her.

'Good baby,' she said. 'What a good baby!'

'He's not a baby,' Leila corrected her. 'He is one and a half.'

Jeanette was so pleased with Pup she wiped his face, picked him up and carried him to show the other hostess what a lovely smile he had.

Ben and Leila examined their food tray. Each contained a cream plate on which sat a white fish shape in a calm sea of scalloped carrot rings and peas. A slice of green pimento stuffed olive represented a bloodshot eye.

Leila started with the tail and worked up to the head peeling off the eye and eating it separately. 'It's tasty,' she declared. Ben picked at the peas one at a time. There was a bird-like delicacy to his movements, repetitious and mesmerising. While Leila spooned apple crumble into her mouth Ben was mashing the fish.

'Don't you like it?' Leila asked. 'I'll have it if you don't want it.'

Ben held on to his plate. 'I do want it.'

He was re-fashioning the fish into a cruel shape of a face with peas for eyes and a sliver of carrot for a mouth. An arrow of chives valentined through his head. 'Who is that supposed to be?' Leila asked.

'Its Dad,' Ben said.

'Dad! That's not Dad, he hasn't got any hair.' She stabbed at the shape with her fork, 'or proper ears or a nose or.... anything.' She reduced the man into a mash.

Ben punched her arm and she screamed, 'That's not Dad!' and punched him back. The food fell on to the floor.

Jeanette was cross with them all the way to Paris. There were no more sweets or gifts.

She made Ben sit alone on the back seat and moved Leila and Pup next to a nun who wore blue tinted glasses and did not look up even when Pup tugged at the pearly beads falling like bad teeth from her waist.

COLD DOGS

Serves 6

Frankfurters
1 kilo (2 lb) potatoes
2 large eggs
Salt
Oil for frying

Peel and finely grate the potatoes. Put them into cold water and then squeeze them dry. Beat the eggs lightly with salt, add to the potatoes and stir well.

Heat the oil in a frying pan. Take serving spoonfuls of the mixture and drop into the hot oil. Flatten a little and lower the heat. When one side is brown, turn over and brown the other. Lift out and serve hot with steaming frankfurters.

It was darkening when they arrived but the snow on the ground gave the streets and roads an eerie cold back light. This was the first time the children had seen snow.

At first Leila thought it might be cotton wool. Ben vaguely recollected illustrations in a book when sitting on his mother's lap: a thin girl with gold plaits in a tattered dress pulling a sledge in a winter storm. 'Don't be stupid, it's white rain.'

'Snow,' Jeanette said. 'Haven't you seen snow before? How hilarious!'

She led them through the lobby of a hotel of fat sofas and deep carpets. It was too late for children in the dining room. She argued with the head waiter and then said. 'Oh do shut up you silly twerp.'

'About turn,' she said to the children. They followed her through the soft carpets and shiny islands of marble.

Jeanette sat them on a bench by the porter's desk. 'Don't move,' she commanded. The porter watched them with a suspicious eye and after a while approached and inspected the name labels Jeanette had pinned to their coats and then returned to his desk to read a newspaper.

'Who likes mustard?' Jeanette asked on her return. She held up a paper bag. 'Din- dins.'

The smell from the bag reminded Leila of a meal her mother had prepared and which had caused her father to shout. 'I don't eat pig!' He had tipped the plate of rust brown steaming sausages onto a newspaper, bundled it tight and told Leila to take it outside to the rubbish bin. 'Not in this house,' he was shouting.

Her mother was saying. 'It's frankfurters! Everybody eats frankfurters!'

She claimed the frankfurters, wrapped in crackly grey paper and a tin of sauerkraut, were a present from a cousin she had been to visit. The children's father laughed bitterly. 'Cousin! Every passing man is your cousin!'

'We know about your cousins,' Leila could hear him shouting again as she ran with the parcel to the rubbish bin. Her hand was warm from holding the parcel. She had to stand on her toes to tip back the lid and as she did so the parcel opened and a sausage fell out. A cat lurking by the bins ambled over to inspect it.

'No,' Leila told it. 'It's not for you' and picked up the sausage and lobbed it into the bin. Her hand was greasy as she threw another and then a third in after it. The smell of the sausages made her mouth water. She wiped her lips with the back of her fingers and tasted the salty smoky flavour. With the cat eyeing her reproachfully Leila gobbled down a whole sausage and then another before tipping the remaining three to the waiting cat.

All there was left to eat in the house was sauerkraut and bread. Ben and his father refused their sauerkraut and ate the bread with salt and the last cucumber in a jar. The children's father said to his wife: 'Nobody likes your food.' Leila saw that her mother was upset so she forked shreds of the tangled sauerkraut into her mouth until she was so full up with it she thought her face would explode.

'Up we go,' Jeanette opened the wrought iron doors of a small lift. 'Breathe in. It's going to be a squeeze. The children followed her along red and green carpeted corridors interspersed with ornamental Chinese pot pourri containers. 'Allez, allez,' she said clapping her hands. She was animated, her mouth smiley and good natured again.

Jeanette handed each child a hot dog wrapped in a crusty bread roll. 'Eat up,' she said. 'Yum yum .' Leila said she didn't like sausages. Jeanette said 'Okey dokey petalkins, pop your sausage back into the bag and just eat the roll.' Leila ate the roll and Ben ate both sausages.

They were all to sleep together in a huge bed with bolsters and white sheets and a fawn eiderdown embroidered with the hotel's crest. Jeanette searched in their case:

' No jimjams, no toothbrushes! Dear oh dear.'

She showed them how to clean their teeth with their index finger.

'Down to your undies, hurry, Jeanette's got a dinner date. With a pilot,' she confided as she tucked them in 'From the Belgian Congo.'

If they were good, and went to sleep straight away, she promised, she'd bring them back some chockies.

WASHED LAMB AND LENTILS

Serves 6

1 ½ kilos (3 lbs) lamb stewing meat (shoulder, breast, ribs, scrag end of neck - a combination of cuts will provide the most interesting texture and sauce)
2 - 3 tablespoons cooking oil
25 g (1 oz) flour
1 tablespoon granulated sugar
Salt
Pepper
500 ml (1 pint) lamb or beef stock or beef bouillon
350 g (3/4 lb) ripe red tomatoes, peeled, seeded and chopped or 3 tablespoons tomato puree
2 cloves mashed garlic
1 bay leaf
6 carrots cut into 3.5 cm (1½ inch) lengths
6 turnips cut into 3.5 cm (1 ½ inch) lengths
15 peeled baby onions with a cross cut in the root end
Green or Puy lentils simmered in salted water until almost tender

This stew can be made in the morning and finished half an hour before dinner time.

Preheat oven to 450F/ 232C/ Gas mark 8
Remove excess fat from meat and cut into 5 cm (2 inch) cubes and dry them. If there are any bones left in the meat leave them there for flavour and remove later. Brown the chunks a few at a time in oil in a frying pan. As they are browned place them in a large casserole. Sprinkle sugar over the lamb and toss over a moderate heat for 3 or

4 minutes. Add salt, pepper and flour and heat in oven for 5 minutes. Toss the meat and return to the oven for another 5 minutes.

Remove casserole, pour out fat and turn oven down to moderate (350F). Put the stock in the frying pan, bring to the boil and scrape up the sauté juices. Pour the liquid into the casserole. Bring to simmering point for a few seconds shaking and stirring to mix the liquid and flour. Add the tomato, garlic, thyme and bay leaf. Simmer for 1 minute.

Place the casserole in the lower part of the oven, cover and simmer for one hour. Then pour the contents into a sieve placed over a bowl. Remove any bones from the lamb and skim the fat off the sauce. Return the lamb and sauce to the bowl and correct seasoning.

Place the carrots, turnips and onions between and around the pieces of lamb and baste with the sauce. Return covered to the oven for half an hour. Add the lentils and simmer in the oven for a further half an hour or until vegetables are tender.

The rented terraced house in Shepherds Bush Green was small with a brown door. 'Where is the Green?' Leila asked. Instead of fields and lines of orange trees there were lines of roads and always people. Wherever you went there were people: in the chilly early mornings men in groups walking fast to work; women in coats in twos and threes at bus stops. Later, clusters of children in uniforms heading for school and mothers with small children, pushing prams, carrying large bags on their way to the shops and markets.

'Where is the bush?' Leila wanted to know. Was it the leggy hedge fronting the house next door or the collection of sickly dusty shrubs studding a stretch of dog-dirtied grass on the main road? And what happened to the shepherd? Her mother explained the bush was chopped down long ago. As for the shepherd he was probably run over by a bus, so be careful how you cross the roads.

The parents were together again and now it was the mother who was well and the father who was having troubles. Mrs Adon worked in a hospital helping the nurses. 'She likes to work with lunatics,' the children's father laughed. He could not find work and gambled at the dogs and at all night card games in houses of men who had more money and card skills. He would return in the early hours distraught.

'The black queen, she got me again,' he had woken Ben to tell him about his bad luck. Leila, from the bed she shared with Pup, had heard his return too and joined her father and brother in the kitchen in the fantasised expectancy that this time his arms would be laden with presents from his winnings - dresses and books and toys, and flowers and money for her mother and wonderful things to eat.

'He lost,' Ben said before she could ask.

Their father said, 'Don't make a noise or your mother will start.'

He had brought something for them however. From his coat pocket he fetched out a blood sodden parcel. A gift from the woman in whose house the gaming had taken place - six pieces of stewing lamb.

'She liked me,' he said. 'When she saw I lost all my money she asked what will your children eat? She gave me her husband's food. He will be furious,' he laughed, 'when he finds out why he is eating meat from a tin tonight.'

It was still dark outside when Mr Adon announced he would begin to prepare the meat. Lamb liked to be cooked twice, to sit in the comfort of its own juices before being heated a second time just before eating. He involved the children in the cooking like a circus master. First the meat must be salted; this he left for Leila to do.

'Not too much!' he warned as she reached for the red and white packet. He watched her sprinkle it on the meat - a little more, a little more. Exactly! The meat must sit in the salt while the vegetables are prepared.

He told Ben to put on his glasses before slicing two onions and to be careful with the knife. Leila's next job was to clean grit and other foreign matter from lentils.

He would wash the soil from the celery and carrots, because this had to be done very very carefully or the food will be ruined. There was no oil or pepper for the meat. No matter, Mr Adon said, there is no hurry. When the shop is open we will obtain oil and pepper, this dish was no good without pepper, pepper gives it character. Character is contrasts: the sweetness of the meat, the heat of the pepper, the fat of the meat, the softness of the lentils, the sharpness of the lemon.

Cooking is like singing. A man who cannot cook is a voice that cannot sing. Limited. If you can cook you have the secret to life, for who does not need to eat? Men are better cooks than women. Why? Because women are always thinking of tomorrow, what will we eat tomorrow? They ration, they compromise.

'Me, I give one hundred and one per cent. Because when I cook I want to make the best for my children: not a meal, a feast.'

'What rubbish,' the children's mother said. She was in the doorway in a discoloured pale yellow candlewick dressing gown, her feet in her street shoes. 'What rubbish are you making now?' she asked.

'Lamb with lentils with rice with onions and herbs. It will be a feast,' he promised.

'You woke me up, me and the children with this smell. Where have you been all night?' She filled the kettle. She had to be at work soon. Who else would bring money to feed them? Not him.

Mr Adon picked up the lamb in the dish and thrust it forward for her to inspect. 'I have brought food, good food for everyone, so shut your mouth. You cannot buy better than this, the best lamb.'

It looked as if at any moment he might throw the lamb at her in his anger so she took the dish from him and inspected it closely and then she laughed her tinny little laugh.

'It's soap, covered in soap.'

Confusing it with salt Leila had sprinkled soap powder on the meat. The packets were similar.

'So much for your wonderful feast,' Sabina Adon's German accent was now strangely overlaid with artisan London. 'And now what will we eat tonight because I don't have nothing left until they pay me.'

She made weak tea and cut bread and spread white margarine and sprinkled it with sugar for breakfast and told the children to get dressed for school. She wasn't speaking directly to her husband, nudging him with her elbows as she passed, not looking at him.

When she was angry with someone she did not see them, they did not exist.

The children returned from school that day to a wonderful smell of lamb and spices. Their father carefully spooned a portion of the meat on to each of their plates.

'I don't eat soap,' Mrs Adon withdrew her plate from the table. She had brought home a tin of spam and a tin of peas for supper. 'Taste before you talk,' Mr Adon said, 'Taste.'

No one moved. At last Leila spooned the lamb and lentils into her mouth. 'It has been washed ten times,' her father said in encouragement. 'Tell them there is no soap.'

Leila chewed. And finally she swallowed.

'There is no soap,' she pronounced.

SEMOLINA SOUP

This recipe has been lost, perhaps existing only in a faulty recollection.

There was trouble with the landlord who said they had to get out. Mr Adon had met a woman with connections who thought she could arrange accommodation with a charity. It would mean living in a building attached to a cemetery which in Victorian times had housed a man and his tools for keeping the grounds in order.

The children's mother said: 'I am not living in no graveyard. You can tell that to the bitch.'

'The rent is free,' Mr Adon was bewildered by his wife's attitude.

'Nothing is free!' Mrs Adon screamed throwing plates on the floor. 'I can smell her on you.'

He shook his head sadly. 'You are truly mad,' he declared.

The floors of the building in the cemetery were bare cement. There was a shallow sink with a cold tap in the entrance passage and an old cooking range in a scullery. Otherwise it was empty. The lavatory was outside next to an unused shed against which leant an ancient garden roller. When Ben pulled it away to open the shed the door fell off its hinges. Inside the cobwebbed dark were mouldering sacks, sticky rotted rubber boots and rusted garden implements, a broken wooden rake and mouse droppings.

The parents went to the second hand shop and returned with a vanful of furniture, Mr Adon sitting next to the driver, Mrs Adon squashed on his lap. The children had been left behind to clean the house. Ben tied a cloth around a garden broom and stretching on a wooden box was able to clear the ceilings of cobwebs. The walls were dingy, speckled with mould. Wiping with the wet broom smeared and made them worse.

Leila suggested they wash the floors to get rid of the dust. Ben tried to attach a length of garden hose to the tap but it leaked so he used a zinc bucket from the shed to throw water on to the floor while Leila brushed away the puddles.

'That's enough,' she kept saying as the puddles grew larger on the uneven floor. She could not keep up with her brother's bucket throwing which had somehow escalated out of control and when he accidentally threw a bucket of water over her shoes she hit him with the broom.

Ben was still attempting to mop up when the parents returned to find the floors flooded. Mr Adon started shouting. Mrs Adon sat on the wooden box and cried. The furniture they had been able to buy was ugly and broken. It would never be mended. Except for cooking and card dealing Mr Adon was not good with his hands. It took days for the moisture to disappear and there was a marshy smell in the house for the remainder of the winter.

The children played chase and hide and seek in the grave-yard until two men knocked on the door and informed their parents this was not allowed.

'You can't have children treading on the dead.'

Soon afterwards Ben joined a boys' club where he learnt boxing and football and Leila joined a girls' club and did painting and table tennis.

In the mornings the premises of the club were used as a children's nursery and during the day elderly people came for a cooked lunch and to play cards and listen to music and talks.

Heidi, the woman who ran the kitchen and canteen there, asked for volunteers. Her regular helper had not arrived. Leila and two others girls making papier maché puppets were given aprons which reached the floor and had to be tied twice round the waist.

Heidi was a refugee and had a limp and a foreign accent. 'We make soup,' she announced, 'to give our old people vigour and strength.' A sinkful of carrots, parsnips and turnips waited to be scrubbed and diced. Celery hearts and onions had to be sliced, parsley chopped. A bag of chicken feet and carcasses were thrown into a stockpot with the vegetables and put on to simmer. 'Tomorrow,' Heidi told them, 'we shall remove all solid parts and add milk and semolina.'

Leila made a face. Semolina in soup! The girls were anxious to return to the papier maché but Heidi had one more task. They each had to peel four whole bulbs of garlic. These would be boiled with the celery leaves and carrot peelings. The girls made more aghast faces behind Heidi's back. 'This will make consommé for our sick people who cannot come.'

'Garlic stinks,' one of the girls said in a nasal voice, holding her nose.

'Not when it is boiled, I can assure you,' Heidi said. 'It is the finest restorative for illness you will ever find. It will cure anything.'

When Leila arrived home she held up her hands and said to her mother: 'Smell.' Mrs Adon moved her head back, repelled by the odour.

But Mr Adon said, 'Beautiful.' He loved the smell and taste of garlic. Leila told him about the making of the consommé.

'Twelve bulbs or twelve cloves, the little pieces?' her father quizzed her.

'Bulbs, big bulbs.'

His face fell. 'Do you know how much so much garlic costs?'

She did not.

'A bloody fortune,' he said. 'Did she pay you, this woman, to peel her garlic for her?'

'No!'

'Next time she asks you to peel garlic, you put some in your pocket to bring home.'

DIFFERENT DUMPLINGS

Watercress Dumplings

Self-raising flour
Shredded suet
Salt, pepper
Chopped watercress

These dumplings are delicious with boiled salt beef.

Mix self-raising flour with half as much suet, salt, pepper, watercress and enough water to make firm dough. Shape the dough into small balls. Carefully drop the balls into very gently simmering water. If the dumplings start to break up the simmer is not gentle enough. Cook for 15-20 minutes until light and fluffy.

The cookery teacher at the girls' school wore a crisp white overall and a starched voile cook's hat over permed pale hair which under the school's institutional bright lights sometimes made her look like a disgruntled matronly angel. The cookery teacher was called Mrs Prothero. Poised on thin and elegant legs encased at the foot in narrow fitting high heeled shoes she demonstrated the dish of the day.

'Girls,' she instructed, 'sit up and open your notebooks.'

Today she would demonstrate boiled beef and parsley dumplings. This was a technical school and the cookery lessons were rigorously taught. The school itself was divided into trades. There were typists, upholsterers, milliners, nurses. Leila was in with the cooks. She was now thirteen, plump, and set for a career in the catering trade. She was also by now an accomplished liar.

'My father,' she would claim in the playground 'is a managing director.'

Her mother, applying for a loan to buy furniture on hire purchase, had asked her husband: 'What shall I put on the form? They want to know what you do.'

'Put market,' he said. 'Market trader.'

She would not put market. 'Nobody is going to give you anything if you put market.'

'Then put managing director.'

She laughed. 'You are a crazy Joe.'

'I manage and direct myself,' he said. 'It is the truth.'

Other girls had fathers who were crane drivers, rodent inspectors, bricklayers. Leila longed to say that her father was a bus driver. And it was almost true. He had applied for a job as a driver with London Transport. To his resentment and humiliation he had been turned down. 'They even take the blacks!' he raged.

From now on he would give up trying for what his wife called normal work.

His real gift was charming people. In his youth in a different country he had been a self taught tourist guide, escorting visitors to secret parts of the city, raking in a percentage from shop owners of whatever customers he had introduced bought in the way of services and goods.

More recently he had dabbled in the antique trade with mild success. A carpet he found in a second hand shop turned out to be a genuine Bokhara. A painting of women bathing in a reed-edged stream bought from a market stall quadrupled in value in an auction house. Too impatient to make a killing to learn anything in depth he was frequently caught with bad buys. Behind the wardrobe and under his bed were the fakes he had paid too much for. For a while he was a porter for a carpet shop. 'Killing me,' he'd say. 'Breaking my back.'

Currently he was a market trader dealing in any lines he could get hold of on credit - ladies shoes, buttons, ballpoint pens, Venetian glass ornaments. These goods he carried in suitcases on to trains to weekly markets in Ashford, Pitsea and Gravesend. The glass ornaments made the cases so heavy they gave him a rupture.

His children accompanied him in turns to help carry the goods up the stairs to the station and to the market sites.

Even after he had the luck of the Bokhara which enabled him to buy a van in which to transport his goods, Mr Adon cajoled the children to accompany him. He disliked being alone. He was in the habit of talking to complete strangers. Housewives at bus stops, workmen around a hole, policemen on street corners, passengers on trains, engaging them with the intimacies of his life story.

On the van journeys he entertained the children with stories from his own childhood, his feats as a guide and as an escapee from women who wanted to entrap him into matrimony and men who wanted to kill him for falling into the temptation.

Once at the market they would unload and then he'd leave for coffee, to meet a friend, to see what others were selling, what was happening - he could not stay in one place for long. He would return three or four times within the hour to see how business was doing and to bring hot drinks and filled rolls, stamp his feet for a few minutes and disappear again.

One murky autumn afternoon in Pitsea when they were unloading, an elderly man who turned out to be school attendance officer, asked how old Leila was.

Mr Adon shook cold hands with the school inspector, called him sir and my friend and then introduced the girl as his wife.

'Really?' the school inspector seemed sceptical.

Leila moved closer to her father.

'I swear on my life,' her father said. 'Thank you for making my wife so happy that she looks so young for her age. It is better for women than jewels, better than flowers to hear they look young to a handsome man.'

'No doubt,' the inspector said. The mocking look he gave her made Leila ashamed. He had not been taken in. 'Next time it will be reported.'

After that she only accompanied her father to the markets on Saturdays and in the holidays.

The girls in the cookery class were instructed to bring money to supplement the cost of the ingredients. For two successive weeks Leila said she had lost her cookery money. There were several other girls in the class who also regularly 'lost' their cookery money. If you said your parents didn't have the money to give you there would be a note from the headmistress requiring a response. On one such occasion Mr Adon wrote back a letter of such obscenities in every language he had picked up that Leila was summoned to the headmistress's office. 'Is your father quite well?' the headmistress enquired.

'He's got chilblains,' Leila replied, not altogether understanding what the headmistress meant.

'Never ever bring this kind of material into my school again. Do you understand?'

'Yes, Miss.'

'You may go,' the headmistress said 'and close the door behind you.'

Girls who had not brought sufficient or any money for ingredients, Mrs Prothero declared, would make dumplings. The other girls, the ones who had been allocated skirt of beef, onions, carrots, were instructed to share their suet and flour with girls lacking in funds. The girls lacking - there were three of them today- sat by the blackboard while the others began their stews by searing the cubes of beef in dripping, adding vegetables, a bouquet garnie and stock from a huge pot of boiled bones always on the go.

Then Mrs Prothero demonstrated the making of dumplings. The suet had to be fresh, all membrane removed and then chopped very fine. This was worked into the flour with seasoning and herbs. Thyme, parsley and marjoram were all acceptable, perhaps a grating of lemon rind for those who felt adventurous. However for a traditional recipe, and most importantly for the purpose of any examinations, she instructed, waiting for her pupils to note it down in their books, chopped parsley and dried thyme, salt and plenty of pepper were all that was required. Those who were not making stew would boil theirs in stock.

Having completed the demonstration she unrolled the sleeves of her starched white overall, re-buttoned the wrist cuffs, removed her spectacles and announced she would return shortly from a meeting in the Staff room. They had forty five minutes in which to prepare their tasks for marking. Mavis, the class prefect, was to ensure good conduct and safe practice until Mrs Prothero's return.

Leila weighed out the flour and as had been demonstrated, sifted it into a bowl with half a teaspoon of salt and three pinches of fine white pepper. She shared a table with a stew maker called Sally Lanyon. They were not friends. Sally only had one friend, Helen Ruck. They were dubbed by the staff as 'the inseparables' and by the other girls as 'double trouble'. Helen Ruck had been allocated a table as far as possible away from Sally. Nevertheless, the two best friends had mimed and signed to each other throughout the lesson to such an extent that Mrs Prothero ordered Helen to turn her chair towards the door so that the two could not make eye contact.

As soon as the click click of Mrs Prothero's high heels descending the stairs faded, Sally moved her chopping board, plate of ingredients and implements to Helen's table taking her lump of suet with her. Leila went over and asked if she could have some.

'Pay for your own,' said Sally, 'like everyone else.'

'Cheek,' said Helen.

Leila dawdled back to her table. Everyone was chopping their suet. Tip tap tip tap. It sounded like some kind of code. She stirred the sifted flour around with her hands, lifting it, aerating it as instructed by Mrs Prothero, and in the process spilling some onto the table and her shoes, and then, having nothing to do, wandered about the kitchen seeing how the other girls were getting on. They were a morose bunch on the whole. Girls who had failed to get into the elite categories as typists or nurses, and were useless with their hands, generally ended up as cooks.

One of the girls passed her a Polo mint and another, Shelagh, her suet mix as stiff as glue, handed her a jug and said, 'Get us some more milk.' Generally the girls were forbidden to open the fridge door without permission. 'Go on, it's paid for,' said Shelagh. 'Hurry up before she gets back.'

Leila searched in the cabinet fridge and found the milk in a large metal container and filled the jug. Shelagh used a slurp of it and told Leila to return the rest to the fridge. Just then the alert passed along from table to table. 'She's coming, she's coming...'

Leila, caught between Shelagh's table and the fridge, scuttled back to her workspace and not knowing what to do with it tipped the milk into the bowl of flour in front of her. Sally, running back with her pastry board tripped and sent flour and suet flying. However, it was not Mrs Prothero but a porter with a tray of ingredients for the next class who entered.

he said stepping over the mess, 'someone's been elves.'

ero entered the kitchen some five minutes later by which th y had cleared up the mess and the Leila had made and boiled a dumpling.

At the finish of the cooking time the young cooks dished up their endeavours for marking.

'Rather a miniature dumpling,' commented Mrs Prothero as she sampled Sally's efforts. 'But tip top taste and texture. Seven out of ten.'

Leila's dumpling earned one point. Mrs Prothero visibly winced as she cut into it and tasted the tiniest sample 'Odd,' she pronounced. 'What is that strange flavour?'

'Polo,' said Leila.

On the confidential end of year class report Mrs Prothero had written of Leila: 'At times she does not seem to know what she is doing or why she is here.'

BANANA FRITTERS WITH RASPBERRY SAUCE

Bananas
Caster sugar
Brandy

For the batter
250 g (10 oz) sifted flour
2 tablespoons melted butter
150 ml (1/4 pint) beer
200 ml (1/3 pint) water
One egg
1 tablespoon brandy
A pinch sugar
A pinch salt

For the sauce
300g (12 oz) fresh or frozen raspberries
Lemon juice
Water
Sifted icing sugar
2 tablespoons Framboise (optional)

First make the raspberry sauce. Puree the raspberries, lemon juice water and icing sugar. Strain through a nylon sieve.
Mix batter ingredients together. Peel bananas and cut in half lengthways. Steep in sugar and brandy for 30 minutes. Drain, dry with a paper towel, dip in batter, and deep fry in smoking hot fat. Arrange on a baking tray, sprinkle with caster sugar and glaze in a very hot oven. Serve with raspberry sauce.

'I'll be perfectly frank with you,' the Chef said at her interview, 'I don't normally allow women in my kitchen.'

'I don't blame you,' Mrs Adon said peering at a baker's tray of mixed fancies on the floor.

'Too much aggravation. And they can't lift.'

'That's what I say,' Mrs Adon had fixed her eye on a chocolate truffle.

She had insisted on accompanying Leila to the interview. It had been a long time since she had made a trip to the West End. Leila agreed with reluctance. 'All right, but don't wear too much lipstick.'

The Chef in his towering boiled and white starched hat was a robust looking man with a strong thin moustache, brown arms, and deep voice that could shout the saucepans into a tremble.

During the lunchtime rush Leila and the Chef worked together at the hot end of the kitchen. She was in charge of two enormous baths of fat supervising deep fried foods while he tended to the expensive end of the menu - Dover soles, poussins, steaks.

Half a dozen silver service waitresses in black dresses and lace edged white aprons and caps, circled through revolving doors with orders, returning with trays of used crockery and cutlery. They shouted out the orders - two vol au vents peas, chips, Brussels please Chef ...one curry.... one steak medium no mushrooms ...two salads...one apple, one banana fritter... two plaice chips and peas ... still waiting on my trout Chef...'. It all had to be remembered. The Chef did not allow paper evidence that might betray how deeply he was swindling the proprietor.

In the mornings the Chef taught Leila how to skin and scale fish, to hack through the centre of a turbot and divide it into profitable portions. She developed a rash on her wrists and was aware on the bus home that she smelt of fish.

'What have you done with the heads,' the Chef bawled across the kitchen. 'Bring the heads over for my stock.'

One of the waitresses, the frail blonde Margot, had earlier pressed close to Leila by the dank fish tanks and said it would be all right but not to let the Chef see her do it. The Chef was a bastard and was getting back at her for something she was too ashamed to mention to a youngster. She needed the fish heads for her cats and smuggled them out of the kitchen in the silver ice-buckets.

'I'm waiting on those heads, girl!'

The next day there was another incident concerning fish. A customer cutting into fillets of plaice complained that the fish was off. The kitchen stopped as the Chef inspected the plate. The waitress who had taken the complaint had a little smirk on her face. Chefs and waitresses being natural enemies, it would have given her satisfaction to see the Chef in trouble. He made an incision through the batter and stared at the pus yellow mess that emerged. He brought the plate closer to his face and turned towards Leila, standing red-cheeked by the fat baths. She had been frying fish throughout the rush. Three battered fillets of plaice on each plate accompanied by a wedge of lemon and blob of Hollandaise sauce had been the dish of the day.

'You,' he roared, 'come and tell me what this is.'

If the fish was bad it was her responsibility, she had sent it out.

'Taste it,' he ordered.

'Taste it!' She refused.

'It's a banana fritter you've mixed up with the fish, you stupid mare.'

The waitresses were ordered to locate and retrieve the fillet of plaice that must have gone out with a banana fritter and raspberry jam order. They flew out of the kitchen like excited jackdaws whipping away plates from under customer's noses and returned them to the kitchen for the chef's autopsy. The lost fillet of plaice was never discovered either on the returned plates or in the swill bins. Presumably someone had eaten plaice smothered with raspberry sauce without noticing.

The Chef bawled at Leila to clear out of his kitchen. She was buttoning her coat when one of the waitresses said Chef wanted to see her in the office. He was not a hard man. He would give her one more chance to wake her ideas up.

At Christmas the Chef, breathing Guinness, presented Leila with a cock turkey. 'Take that to your mother,' he said. 'It's a Norfolk bird, compliments of the management.'

Leila blinked at the bird. Its blood-clotted purple head drooped back on its body. Its feet, still intact, were soiled with grey mud.

'And what have you got to say to that?'

'It's...it's a bit big.'

'Did you hear that....!'

It became the topic of the day. The Chef couldn't repeat it often enough. 'They're now complaining the turkeys are too big, too bleeding big....'.

The cashier leaving his accounting coop in the restaurant room for a cramped corner behind the cloakrooms for his lunch said: 'I hear the chef's giving away turkeys so big the staff can't carry them.'

At tea time the Chef drove off for a private celebration with the proprietor, a real Lord. Leila was to lock up the premises. In a moment of arrogance she had declared she saw no point in keeping Christmas.

'D'you mean to say you haven't even bought your mum a little present?'

He handed her the keys. 'They won't be long.' The kitchen staff had been sent off early with a turkey and a bottle of claret. The waitresses were finishing up in the restaurant. The tablecloths were tied into bundles, the chairs tipped on to the tables, the cruets returned to the servery.

Leila leaned against the wall and rested one foot on top of the other. Her feet were beginning to swell.

The restaurant was in a semi-basement. From the arched windows she could see as far up as people's knees on the outside. Only dogs and toddlers were viewed complete. Like an animated shoe shop window. Drama from the waist down. Once Leila had seen a man's walking stick lift the skirt of a pair of legs in strappy sandals. Now you couldn't see much. The daylight was dying.

Leila's turkey lay in the chip sink. 'Like a baby,' she thought. 'A deformed baby's body.' She went in search of a cardboard box, a coffin, into which to lay it. Some of the waitresses were now scurrying out.

'Happy Christmas'

'And to you'

'And a happy New Year.'

'And to you.'

It had been going on like this all day. She could hear laughter from the restaurant room. She'd go in and ask them to hurry up. She'd got things of her own to do.

Margot and two of the other waitresses, Rose who was a Catholic but not Irish and little Stella, burst into fresh laughter as Leila stood in the doorway. They were sitting on the bar counter, swinging their legs, each with a bottle of drink.

'Come over here, darling,' Margot called across. 'Join the party.'

Rose now stood on the counter, her shoes in her hands and began to sing a song about a broken heart.

'I want to lock up,' Leila said.

'What she say?'

'She wants to lock up.'

'In a minute darling. Give us a minute.'

'Only five minutes more, only five minutes more...' Margot was now singing.

Leila returned to the kitchen, switched off a few lights and waited and felt morose. It was now dark outside. She'd get stuck in the evening rush. The shops would be closed. The waitresses continued to sing. Leila searched the bins for paper in which to wrap the turkey. They had all been emptied. She heard a crash from the restaurant room.

Rose was lying on her side on the floor stroking the legs of a table and mouthing the words of a song. Margot had stripped off her uniform and was sitting on the counter in beige and pink underwear crying, her scratched arms outstretched.

'We've got to get them home,' Stella said. 'Give us a hand to get them home. We've got to get them into a taxi,' and then lurched over the bar and vomited.

It took Leila almost an hour to dress the waitresses in their coats and move them to the back door of the kitchen. She propped them against each other on the floor and phoned for a taxi.

The taxi driver glanced down at the waitresses, shook his head and returned to his cab without a word. Leila phoned for another.

'Sorry miss, I can't take the chance, they'll be sick all over my cab. Not in that condition. I can't take them in that condition.'

The fourth driver looked like a wrestler.

'What you should do,' he advised, 'is call an ambulance. I wouldn't take them if you gave me a hundred pounds.'

She tried another number.

'Can't do it,' the driver said. He was a small pinched looking man with a greyhound's slant of eyes.

'I want to show you something,' Leila said.

'What's going on round here?' He followed her into the kitchen.

'Something you might be interested in,' she was using father's market stall cajoling voice.

She showed him the turkey.

'It's a beauty,' he was impressed. 'A knockout.'

'You can have it. For nothing. It's a Norfolk bird.'

The driver considered the waitresses. 'You'll have to wrap them up.'

They went in search of tablecloths into which they wound the waitresses before lifting them into the taxi. Leila rummaged through the handbags in search of money for the fare. The driver wanted it in advance. In Margot's bag she came across a fish head in a plastic bag.

She'd found the waitresses' addresses from a list on the Chef's office wall. The first one they tried was Stella's, a basement in Fulham. There was no one in and none of the keys in Stella's handbag fitted the lock.

'I wish I'd never taken this on,' the driver complained. He had placed the naked bird in the back of the cab with the waitresses. 'How long is it going to take to cook, anyway?'

'You can put it overnight in a slow oven. It'll cook itself.'

'I don't even think it's going to fit into our oven. And what about it's head, does that come off before you cook it or after?'

When they opened the door of Margot's flat an army of cats approached.

'I can't bugger about any longer, let's bring them all in here. They can sort themselves out when they come to.'

The waitresses were laid out side by side on a settee. The cats walked across them.

Leila asked the driver to take her to Charing Cross station.

'You got a long way to go?'

'If I can get a train I'll be all right.'

'Not in London then? If it was in London I could oblige you.'

'No, it's in the country.'

When she arrived at the hospital the Matron invited her to join the party.

'We have one every year, our own little Christmas party. Oh and they do so enjoy it, something different, isn't it?'

'Didn't you bring me nothing,' Mrs Adon asked. She was eating a petit four. They'd tied her hair up in green and red ribbons.

'I nearly bought you a turkey,' Leila said.

TURKISH COFFEE

Serves 1

1 heaped teaspoon pulverised medium or dark roast coffee beans
1 teaspoon sugar or to taste
1 cardamom pod

Put the coffee, cardamom, sugar and a small cup of water in a pan. Heat, stirring, and when the coffee starts to rise remove from the heat immediately. Give a quick stir. Boil again and pour into a cup. If you are making several cups share the froth from the first boil.

The room where Leila now lodged was once a workshop in a four storey house. It was approached from the side by unstable wooden stairs. The owners were a couple of elderly Poles who lived below. He was a semi invalid, an ex-manufacturer of ladies' handbags. His wife was wizened, a stunted waxen-faced elderly with bright auburn dyed hair who could not take the stairs to the top floor.

'You go up and make up your mind,' she boomed. She was hard of hearing. 'When you have decided knock on my window loud.'

The room contained a brass bed with a mouldering mattress, a failing Baby Belling cooker on a stand, a chest with one drawer missing, another stuck on broken runners and a huge, handsome, mirror-fronted wardrobe. The washing facilities were a cold tap and a small deep sink behind a curtained off section on the lower landing. There was no bathroom and the lavatory was in the back garden.

'What do you expect for this rent, Buckingham Palace?' the Polish woman asked.

Ben had moved in with students to a semi-derelict house on the other side of London.

'You could brighten it up,' he suggested when he saw the room and the next time he visited brought a bunch of crepe paper carnations in mixed colours.

Returning home on the bus from the kitchen on her afternoon off one sunny day Leila decided to walk some of the way and found herself facing the window of a youth employment office. The office was upstairs and the only occupant was a middle-aged man in a tweed jacket and brown woven tie called Mr H. Boston.

He said take a pew, fill in a form, and then looked through his card index file. There was a vacancy in a hospital as a junior cook. 'Not hospitals,' Leila said.

The Post Office canteen was in need of a vegetable cook.

'Not cooking,' she said.

The sausages factory always had vacancies for linkers.

'Nothing to do with food.'

He fingered the cards and asked about her hobbies, her family, her present occupation, what she was good at. 'I like talking,' Leila said. 'Talking and imagining things.'

He asked if she would like a cup of tea and while they waited for the kettle she told him her father had a passion for black coffee. He never touched anything but real coffee and it had to be strong. The way he made it was to have it ground up very fine like powder. It was even better if you bought the roasted beans whole and then shook them about in a dry pan over the gas ring with a split cardamom seed before grinding them.

Her German grandmother had a coffee grinder. It was attached to the wall and had a ceramic handle decorated with blue flowers. But her father didn't like German coffee. It was too milky. He never drank milk. She didn't ever drink milk either now. She didn't like the smell of it. And how can it be natural for us to drink the milk of other creatures? And if it is natural than why don't we drink dog milk or horse milk or monkey milk? She suddenly stopped talking, aware she had run on too long. She often found herself doing it these days, mostly to strangers, captive audiences at bus stops, shopkeepers behind tills.

Going on and on about disconnected subjects, searching for something to convince, to engage. Unable to pause. He must have thought you were crazy, she told herself afterwards, a crazy girl. Talking rubbish. Unstoppable nonsense.

'So you want your tea without milk,' Mr Boston said after a long pause. The kettle had boiled and he was stirring the pot with a pencil.

'You'll get lead poisoning doing that,' she warned. 'Lead rots your brain.'

'I seem to have lost the spoon,' he said.

She drank her tea and refused a shortbread biscuit on the grounds that the fat they put in biscuits came from whales. She wouldn't mind a job involving animals. But not zoos, she hated zoos. Or an air hostess, she wouldn't mind being an air hostess.

When she finished her tea Mr Boston closed the card index box tapped it a few times and said: 'I'll contact you if anything suitable comes up.'

The next time she came by it was to present him with a spoon she had stolen from the kitchen.

He didn't have a job in mind for her. 'What I think you need,' he said 'is some education.'

RAHAT LOKUM TURKISH DELIGHT

Extraordinarily complicated and difficult - perhaps for making in the imagination.

500 g (1 lb) glucose
2.5 kilos (5 ½ lb) granulated sugar
375 g (¾ lb) corn flour
Juice of 1 lemon
1 teaspoon pulverised mastic
A few drops food cochineal (optional)
3 tablespoons orange blossom water or rose water
75 g (3oz) chopped pistachios
Icing sugar

In a large pan put the glucose, sugar and 500 ml (1 pint) water. Stir well and bring to the boil, stirring from time to time.

In another large pan put the corn flour. Gradually add 1.5 litres (2 ½ pints) water stirring until mixed in. Slowly bring to the boil, stirring until you have a smooth white paste. Slowly add this to the hot sugar mixture, stirring vigorously to prevent any lumps from forming.

Bring to the boil again and cook over a low heat for about three hours or until it reaches the required consistency. To test the correct consistency take a small quantity of the mixture and squeeze it between two fingers. The mixture should cling to both fingers when the fingers are drawn apart leaving gummy threads.

Add the lemon juice, the orange blossom / rose water and cochineal. Grind the mastic with a little granulated sugar and add to the mixture. Stir vigorously and cook for a few more minutes. Stir in the chopped nuts.

Pour the mixture into shallow trays which have been dusted with flour to prevent sticking. Flatten with a knife and leave for twenty four hours. Then cut into squares and coat with sifted icing sugar.

Most of the others in the class were foreigners. The remainder were university entrance failures attempting re-takes. These included a public school boy called Norman Sutherfield who constantly interrupted lectures with complicated questions; a loud Australian girl called Robin; a middle-aged nun who needed English and Geography for an overseas mission, and a mysterious girl called Geraldine who wafted intermittently into lectures beautifully groomed and carrying an ostrich skin brief case. Someone said Geraldine was the illegitimate daughter of a debutante and an East End gangster.

Mr Boston had helped Leila fill in an application form for a grant.

'We'll say your intention is to become a dietician,' he wrote in the details. 'Which means you'll have to do maths, chemistry and biology for your science subjects.'

Leila made a face.

When she told Ben she was leaving the kitchen to become educated he had said, 'Educated as what?'

'As a dietician.'

He had laughed, 'That's a good one.' She didn't understand what the joke was but didn't say so. She and Ben met rarely now. He was associating with other people. 'Well, you know,' he said vaguely when she pressed him to describe his new friends. 'Art students, those kinds, you wouldn't like them.'

She would! What he meant, she really knew, was that they wouldn't like her.

In the biology lab Leila was paired with a vivacious gazelle-eyed Arab girl with shoulder-length hair called Suha. The lesson was to dissect a frog pickled in formalin and to label its digestive and reproductive system. Suha was deft at dissecting. She laid out the parts on the small square of marble. 'Write,' she instructed Leila who was to name the parts on a diagram, 'liver, here, you see his little liver.' Leila peered at the grey blob. The metallic smell of the formalin made Leila feel sick and she fled.

Suha found her in the fluorescent bright canteen sitting alone with a cold cup of black tea. 'What is the matter with you!' she demanded. 'You have to be in class and work. Otherwise what will happen to you?'

'I can't touch dead things,' Leila said.

'We shall go shopping' Suha declared, 'Come.'

As they walked to the shops in Bond Street Suha linked arms with her.

'Talk,' she commanded. 'Anything, say anything,' there was desperation to her voice.

'What are you making your studies for?'

Leila told her about Mr Boston in the employment office.

'Are you in love with him?' Suha asked.

'No!'

Suha was in love with someone, another student at the college, an English boy called Roy. It was a secret. Her people would kill them both if they found out.

At the top of New Bond street Suha gripped Leila's arm tight. 'Walk fast,' she said, her eyes bright with fear. She was being followed. By whom? By relatives, relatives of relatives. She was being watched all the time. 'Don't look back,' Suha hissed as Leila turned to see who it was following.

They walked briskly, dashing to beat the red lights at a crossing.

'Do you live with your family?' Suha asked. Leila told her about her room with the Poles.

'Is it far?' Half an hour on the Underground, longer but cheaper by bus.

'Talk, keep talking,' Suha grasped Leila's elbow and led her into Fenwicks. 'Like we are two normal girls talking about what clothes we will buy.'

'This one will suit you,' Suha picked up mustard yellow boat necked sweater. 'Yes, we will buy this one.' Leila did not have money for sweaters, she did not like the murky colour and it looked too tight.

'No, I don't want it,' she said. But Suha did not seem to hear her. 'It is beautiful.'

In the changing room Suha whispered: 'When we are paying ask me to go to your house to do homework. Ask in a loud voice.' Leila was about to say she did not have a house but Suha shushed her. 'Please,' she whispered, 'Be my friend.'

At the counter Suha nudged Leila who said 'Do you want to come to my place?'

'Your house?' Suha said loudly.

'To do our homework.'

'Yes, we can go now,' Suha said and linked arms with her again.

'So this is the room,' said Suha. She lay back on the bed. 'It's perfect.'

'It's not, it's horrible.'

'Horribly perfect then,' Suha said. 'It's a little cold. Do you have coffee?'

Leila had half a packet of tea and three stale cream crackers.

Suha said never mind. She asked about the Poles.

'Do they mind who you bring here?'

The only person who had visited was her brother. 'I have to put the rent through their letter box every Friday. Otherwise they don't take any notice of me,' Leila said.

After a week only one of the two-bar electric heater gave heat. A day later the other bar went. The Polish woman said all breakages would have to be replaced. 'What have you done to it?'

'Nothing!' Leila protested. 'It broke itself.'

Another day she went down to report that the oven of the Baby Belling did not work. 'So use the hot plate,' the Polish woman said. 'I don't want complaints every five minutes, you don't like the place, find somewhere else.'

Despite protestations Suha persuaded Leila to try on the mustard jumper. 'It looks nice, you keep it, a present from me,' she insisted.

Looking out of the window behind the curtain Suha said in a voice that was cold, almost detached, that in a year her life would be over. She was to return home to marry a member of the diplomatic service.

'Is he nice?'

'Very nice, very rich,' Suha said and began to cry. 'But I don't love him.'

'What will you do?' Leila asked.

'I will go back home and marry him and then my life will be finished. That's how it is.'

'You could run away.'

'There is nowhere to run.'

'But he is kind,' Leila insisted, 'this man you're marrying.'

'He is very kind. Don't worry about it,' Suha said. She had now recovered.

'You should not be afraid of colours. This yellow suits you very much.'

Suha did not come to the college for some days. Leila faithfully continued to attend lectures and take copious notes of algebraic terms and chemistry formulas she did not understand. Her homework was returned with enormous questions and exclamation marks 'What is this?' and 'No mark possible'. She did a little better with other subjects. The biology lecturer returned a paper on glands of the human body with instructions not to dress the outlines in clothes. English essays attracted enigmatic remarks. 'Off track but imaginative.' Not knowing what to say about *'A Day in the Country'* Leila had explained how to make a meal with one olive.

'I have been to Paris,' Suha declared catching up with Leila in the college entrance hall.

She placed her hand on Leila's shoulder and chatted all the way up the stairs to the library. She had stayed with a cousin who had an apartment in the heart of Paris overlooking the Seine. 'Have you ever been to Paris?' Suha asked.

'Oh yes,' Leila said, 'I stayed in a posh hotel.'

At eleven a.m. they were due in the biology lab in another building.

'Stay,' Suha urged tugging at Leila's sleeve. 'Roy wants to meet you. Just ten minutes.'

Suha gathered her own books and left. A moment later a stocky young man in a Fair Isle sweater sat opposite Leila. He looked disgruntled. 'What a game,' he said and sighed. His sea-green eyes looked her over. 'Where d'you want to go,' he asked wearily. 'Anywhere in particular?'

She wanted to go to her class. 'I'm supposed to be in biology,' she said.

'What about a pub?'

'I don't go into pubs.' He made a face.

He took her to a cafe in a department store and asked what she wanted to eat. Leila said she didn't mind. He left her at a table and returned with a fizzy orange drink and a wedge of cake for her and a cup tea and cold sausage roll for himself.

'What's that like?' he asked as she ate into the cake.

'It's all right.'

'It's supposed to be coffee cake

'I know,' Leila said. 'I've had it before.'

'So what do you think of Suha?'

'She's nice.'

'She's bloody wonderful. She wants us to be friends. You do know why don't you?'

'Not really.'

'Work it out.'

'She said she was being watched.'

He took her hand and kissed it with mock gallantry. 'Exactly.'

Both Suha and Leila passed the biology test which was to map the course of the human heart and colour the ventricles in red and the auricles in blue.

'You like my Roy, don't you!' she was animated, urging Leila for the right answer. Just a little bit?'

Leila shrugged.

'When you know him better, you will love him. He is a truly wonderful person.'

'He is not my type,' Leila said.

'Please be my friend,' Suha took her hand and held it. 'Please like my Roy.'

Suha had some presents for her from Paris. Real coffee, a brass coffee maker and brown sugar crystals.

The coffee Suha prepared in Leila's room was aromatic and strong. They tested each other on the respiratory system. Leila asked Suha what she was studying for.

'I told you, to be the wife of a diplomat you have to know something.' Suha lay on the bed and patted it. 'Lie down by me,' she said. 'I am so cold.'

The next day after Geography in which they did Artesian wells and the Thames Basin Roy was waiting for Leila. 'Ready sweetheart?' he said. 'We're going to the flicks.'

It was a daytime showing in Brixton of Alan Ladd in 'Shane'. Afterwards he insisted on seeing her home. 'Ask me in,' he said. 'Invite me for a coffee.'

Suha arrived half an hour later with her books and a carrier bag.

'Fruit,' she said producing a melon and grapes 'and for you, my friend - here, take it. Take it.'

Leila opened a padded rectangular box. Layers of fine translucent paper enclosed little pillows of delicately coloured, powdered sugar. Turkish Delight.

'Can you give us a few minutes?' Suha asked.

Leila sat on the landing eating the Turkish Delight until it was too cold to sit any longer. She went upstairs to knock on her door and heard sounds she was too embarrassed to interrupt. She tiptoed down the stairs again and sat on the landing. When it was almost dark Roy came skipping down the stairs and tossed Leila's coat and scarf at her.

'See me to the bus stop,' he said draping his arm on her shoulder.

They walked to the bus stop without a word. As the bus approached he kissed her cheek and said. 'You can go now.'

When she returned to the room Suha was making coffee.

'I'm not doing it again,' Leila mumbled.

Suha said she understood. Her tone was cold and she did not look directly at Leila. She asked if she could stay for another half hour so that whoever was watching would not suspect that Roy was Suha's and not Leila's friend. They did no talk about it any more.

Suha ate the remainder of the Turkish Delights as they sat on the bed and revised anatomy.

The next time Roy approached Leila she told him to buzz off.

'Gone off the sweeties have we?' his snort was contemptuous.

Shortly afterwards Leila left the college to work in a cigarette factory. She did not like being there any more and her funds for that term had run out.

Waiting on a platform for a train home one evening after a long shift Leila met the nun. The nun told her that Geraldine had tragically passed away. She had registered at the college knowing she had only a short time to live before she joined all the saints and angels in heaven. It was something to preoccupy herself with while she waited. She also revealed that Suha was now married.

'Her folks took her back home quick march when they discovered she was carrying on with someone inappropriate.'

'How did they find out?' Leila asked.

'She was far too open about it apparently, and they have eyes everywhere.'

The nun was off to Kampala soon. 'You'll write to me, from time to time, won't you?'

'Of course,' Leila said without interest, as her train arrived. She wanted to cry but did not quite know why. For Geraldine. For Suha, for her own part in Suha's story.

The nun pressed a card on her. 'This address will always find me.'

EGGS VOILÀ!

Trim the crusts off a slice of white bread. Cut out a circle (preferably with a biscuit cutter) in the centre.

In a hot frying pan melt a little butter and oil. Into it place the bread and press with a spatula or spoon. When is browned on one side turn it over and carefully slide a fresh egg into the circle. Season the egg with salt and peer and baste with the fat until the white is cooked to your liking. Serve on a hot plate with salted halved grilled tomato.

On a wintry day Leila met Ben on the steps of the National Gallery. He looked gaunt and cold in a grubby grey hooded coat. Like a moulting fox, she thought.

'Where's Dad?' she asked.

Mr Adon was in a corner cafe flirting with a tall waitress.

'Bring coffee for my children my darling,' he called to the waitress across the assortment of plastic padded chairs. 'She is a beauty, she is a lovely,' he said loud enough for the waitress and other customers to hear, so open about it none could take offence.

The cafe was used by cab drivers who nipped in for fresh filled rolls and a quick mug of steaming tea. They stood at the counter, stamping their feet for warmth as they waited for their orders.

'How are you my darling daughter,' Mr Adon said, his eyes on the waitress's long legs.

'I've got a job,' Leila said, 'in a cigarette factory.'

She was in the inspection department. Double glazed and dimmed and kept at a stable humidity to protect the quality of the tobacco, it was like being enclosed in the membrane of an egg. In the mornings, attired in a white overall, clip board and pencil in hand, her duties were to wander between rows of tall shelving on which loose cigarettes awaited packing, randomly selecting batches of twenty five cigarettes at a time and weighing them on small brass balance scales, entering the weight on a form. In the afternoon she wafted among the shelving, selecting five cigarettes from random batches, inserting each into a calibrator to ascertain the diameter.

At the end of each shift the forms were taken to an office a half flight up from the inspection floor. There Leila deposited them into a cardboard box on a bench outside the manager's office. An empty box appeared each morning. Leila assumed her forms were examined and assessed, but after a while she wrote in imaginary figures on the forms.

Occasionally on her way down from the manager's floor, Leila wandered into the export packing department where girls similarly bored by the repetitive tasks also took strange risks. Tins of cigarettes destined for the armed forces and Royal Navy sometimes contained lewd messages inserted by girls playing a variation of cigarette roulette. The packs were traceable to each operator. The discovery of a message meant instant dismissal.

'What is it you do there in the factory?' her father asked Leila.

'It's quite interesting,' she lied. 'I inspect the cigarettes.'

'You are an inspector of cigarettes!'

'It's better than nothing.'

'Don't talk rubbish,' he said. 'Do something with your life. You can cook. Find a man to marry.'

Mr Adon was now on the road on commission as a rep for a fountain pen company.

Business was terrible. Nobody was interested in handwriting any more.

They wanted to give him a Northern region. He didn't want to go. 'North is cold. I hate the cold. And anyway from time to time I must see your mother. She is mad, of course. When the doctors said she can go home she refuse. She likes it with the mad people. That is how they prove she is still mad.'

Ben was doing something with his life. He was studying to be an artist. Mr Adon was meeting him with a proposition. There was a cardboard suitcase by his chair.

'Here,' he said, 'look at this. This is how you can make money.' He had acquired three scores of assorted plain rayon ties very cheaply. He wanted Ben to paint them.

'What do you mean paint them?'

Mr Adon took a folded magazine from his coat packet. He was about to open it.

'Go and choose a cake for yourself,' he said to Leila. 'A doughnut, anything you like.'

'I'm not hungry,' she said.

'Get something for me to eat in the van later. Go, I want to show your brother something.'

Ben carefully took out his spectacles from a rigid case and peered at the magazine. Naked women riding impossibly white horses, naked women coyly bending over to play with a kitten, ladies in mortar board hats, high heels and nothing else.

'Paint pictures like this on the ties, we make a fortune. I know a man who will buy as many as you can make.'

At the counter Leila watched the stunted, balding Sicilian counter-hand make up a hot bacon sandwich for a cab driver.

'Have you got any hot dogs,' she asked.

'We have hot dogs, we have saveloys, we have bangers, we have frankfurters, with, without mustard, HP, tomato sauce, onions, without onions, anything you like.'

'Frankfurters,' she said, 'with English mustard.'

'More,' she said, as the counter hand squirted mustard on the sausage. 'A lot more.'

On the way to the bus Leila asked Ben what it was her father did not want her to see.

'His cheap dreams.'

'What do you mean? What are you talking about?'

'He's a dreamer, like you.'

'I'm not!'

'A dreamer schemer.'

She was in a sulky mood, accusing him of neglecting her.

'You never tell me things. You never ask me to your place. You never introduce me to your friends. You never come to my place. You never take me out. We never do anything together.'

'You can come to my place,' he said, 'I'll cook you something.'

Cooking was Leila's territory. 'You can't cook.'

It was the first time she had visited her brother's flat. It was on the second floor of a three storey house about to be demolished to make way for council flats. There was refuse in the front garden and the windows of the ground floor were boarded up.

The furniture in the sitting room was arranged close to the walls. On a stained carpet in the centre was an orange box on which stood a chipped wine glass.

'Whatever happens, don't walk across the room,' Ben warned. The floor was in danger of collapse.

He proposed to leave her there to look through a film magazine while he prepared the meal. 'If the glass moves, make your way out as fast and as lightly as you can.'

'Let me help you,' she said.

He wanted the meal to be a surprise.

'I won't look then,' she promised.

'And don't talk, I need to concentrate.'

The kitchen was narrow, wedged between the bathroom and another bedroom. It was greasy and smelt of mouldering raw onions. Leila sat at a small table under a window overlooking a dank garden and watched a ginger cat covering up a patch it had soiled.

'Is that your cat?' she asked.

'Don't look,' Ben instructed. The cat belonged to the tenant below, a civil servant working for the Admiralty.

'Where are the other people you share with?' she asked.

'They won't be here until later.' She heard him crack an egg.

'Are they nice? Can I meet them?'

'Look, I need to concentrate.'

There was smoke in the room and the sound of sizzling. Leila smelt fried egg and rancid fat.

'Guess what I ordered for Dad's sandwich,' she said.

Ben did not respond, he was engrossed in the cooking.

'He never takes any notice of me,' Leila ran on. The cat below was slinking away.

'You can turn round now,' Ben said. 'Voilà!'

'Voilà?'

'It's French. What do you think?'

On a white plate sat a precisely cut square of bread fried to a burnished gold. Cut out of the centre was a perfect circle into which an egg had been gently dropped and fried until the top was set.

Leila cut into the greasy bread and pierced the yolk.

'What do you think?' Ben asked again.

She thought it's a fried egg with greasy fried bread. She said. 'Marvellous, where's yours?'

He was eating later with the students in the house. She wanted to meet them but Ben said you will, you will, another time. He switched on the radio to check the time. He didn't want her to travel after dark.

'It's dark already,' she protested as he held her coat out for her.

WATERCRESS SALAD

A Perfect Green Salad

Serves 4
3 - 4 little gem lettuces
1 bunch watercress

½ clove garlic

Salt
1 tablespoon wine vinegar
6 tablespoons extra virgin olive

Crush the garlic with the salt. Whisk in the vinegar and then the oil. Wash and dry the lettuce and watercress. Toss the leaves in the dressing a few minutes before eating.

Mrs Adon had said, go and visit my aunt, she would like to see you. Leila rang the telephone number several times and left messages with a cleaner.

'Did you call my aunt?' Mrs Adon asked on each visit. One day Leila called and the aunt herself answered. 'What is it you want?' she asked in a German voice.

'Nothing,' Leila said. 'My mother wants me to visit you.'

'How is your mother?'

'She's all right.'

'Good. And your father?'

'He's away.'

'Away?'

'I could see you any Sunday' Leila said. 'Or any evening.'

'And your brothers - how are your brothers?'

When Mrs Adon was first ill Pup was taken to stay with a family in the country. Two women came in a car to drive him there.

'It will be better for the little lad. Just until things settle,' one of them said. The other had kept her unsmiling eyes on Leila.

Leila possessed a photograph of herself in Trafalgar Square carrying Pup. Ben was in the picture backing away from a fluttering out-of-focus pigeon and her parents were behind them. On the back of the photograph her mother had written in fountain pen 'The family and Pigeons, Trafalgar Square, London'

They were still living together in the house in Shepherds Bush when Leila, while washing plates, had asked her father if they could visit the country one day to see her little brother.

Mr Adon shouted. 'Don't talk about it! I don't want to hear about it from you, from anybody, anymore!' He had been dicing vegetables for a lentil soup. He continued to cube the carrots and then started weeping.

'Don't,' Ben patted his father's arm. Mr Adon pushed him away and threw the knife on the floor and walked out of the kitchen. Ben picked up the knife.

'You're so naive,' he said, placing the knife in a drawer and closing it.

'I'm not naive!' Leila did not know what it meant but it sounded uncomplimentary.

'You don't know what's going on.'

'I do!'

'You don't know what's going on because you don't think. And you don't listen.'

'What is going on? How can I know if you don't tell me? Tell me.'

'You already know.' She denied it.

'I'll ask dad, if you won't tell me.' Ben pushed her away from the door.

'He's been adopted.'

'What do you mean adopted!'

'Don't pretend you don't know.'

Leila realised she did know, but somehow had forgotten.

The aunt had prepared a little meal - thin overlapping slices of speckled meat lay alongside halved boiled eggs decorated with specks of fish roe. Radishes shared a cut glass bowl with fingers of celery and bunchlets of watercress.

'Young maidens must eat much watercress.'

The aunt used wooden salad servers to pile Leila's plate. 'Watercress contains iron. And how is your mummy these days?' Leila reported that her mother was improving. She was doing knitting and making a tray.

'She is better where she is,' the aunt said. 'Where there are kind people to look after her.'

Leila resented this, but said nothing. She was chewing the salty meat - and something else that she was having difficulty in breaking down.

'You know the best dressing for a watercress salad, its walnut oil. Would you care for a little more?'

Leila continued chewing. By now she had deduced that the item in her mouth giving her trouble was the elastic band that had held the watercress bunch together.

'You know,' the aunt was saying, 'your mother was always a handful. Always wayward. But you are not like that, I can see. You are a sensible person. What is it you are doing?'

Leila told her she had just been accepted for a job in publishing.

'You don't say!'

'Yes,' Leila continued to chew, waiting for a suitably discreet moment to withdraw the elastic band from her mouth. The aunt asked her if she would like a little more meat, a little more salad, there was so much and one didn't want to be wasteful.

Leila shook her head. The rubber in her mouth was becoming irksome.

'Would you like something to drink now?' Leila nodded, hoping this would provide a chance for her to dispose of the elastic band. But the aunt had already made up a jug of coffee in a thermos.

'Do you like it black or do you like it white?' the aunt asked as she poured the coffee into fragile china cups looking straight at Leila.

Leila swallowed the elastic band and said, 'Black. Please.'

BALLS OF FIRE

Meatballs in Tomato Sauce

For the Tomato Sauce
1 large clove crushed garlic
2 tablespoons olive oil
1 teaspoon sugar
1 tablespoon balsamic vinegar
1 small dry chilli, crumbled
2 teaspoons oregano
2 tins good quality chopped tomatoes
1 handful fresh basil
Salt and pepper
2 - 3 tablespoons extra virgin olive oil

For the Meatballs
1 kilo (2 lb) minced meat
1 handful white breadcrumbs
2 teaspoons dried oregano
1 teaspoon caraway seeds, slightly crushed
1 tablespoon chopped fresh rosemary
1 onion
1 clove chopped garlic
1 tablespoon mustard
1 egg
4 tablespoons olive oil
Lots of fresh basil
60 g (2 - 3 oz) mozzarella in pieces
60 g (2 - 3 oz) grated parmesan

First make the tomato sauce: gently fry the garlic in a heavy-based pan, and then add the chilli, tomatoes and oregano. Boil and simmer for one hour. Then mix in the vinegar, sugar, basil, extra virgin olive oil and seasoning.

For the meatballs: Fry the onion until golden then add the garlic and cook for a few seconds. Blend together the meat, breadcrumbs, herbs, spices, mustard, egg and seasoning. Make balls the size you like, roll in flour and in a casserole dish fry on both sides until browned. Remove from heat, add the tomato sauce basil and cheeses and cook in the oven at 400F/ 200C / Gas mark 6 for 15 -20 minutes until the cheese is a golden colour.

'I'm having a dinner party,' Leila announced to Ben 'Would you like to come? You can bring a friend.' They were travelling back on the train from visiting their mother.

'A dinner party!'

'You don't have to come,' she said. 'It's just an idea.'

She had only just thought of it. She brightened at the notion of folding napkins and handing round cheese and biscuits. She would search the market for second hand cups and cutlery. She might buy a bunch of grapes.

She recalled one of the lessons in the cookery class, 'Planning a Dinner Party for Six.' She had copied and underlined Points to Remember from the blackboard. Dishes to avoid - those requiring last minute preparation; those spoilt by waiting; those you have not tried previously. Beware of over elaboration was the final edict; a simple dish well made and attractively served will suffice.

'What are you going to cook?' Ben asked.

'Wait and see,' she said.

'Who else is coming?'

'Some friends.'

'You haven't got any chairs.'

'We can sit on the bed. Or on the floor. It's going to be casual.'

'So I won't need to dress up,' Ben said and raised his hand to add, 'Joke, joke,' to save her the embarrassment of realising he was mocking her.

Leila sent invitation cards to Mr Boston from the employment office, the nun and Robin, the Australian girl whom she met by chance in the Strand on her way to the National Gallery. Robin was returning to Southern Australia. She invited the Leila to come out and visit her there one of these days.

Leila looked up recipes in the library and considered in turn Beef Olives, Navarin of Lamb, Stuffed Hearts. She finally decided on a Coq Au Vin but on the day she set out to the butcher the She-Pole lay in wait for her.

Leila promised rent settlement by the end of the week. 'No excuses. No rent, no room,' the She-Pole raised her voice.

'You can have a pound of mince,' the butcher said when she asked him what was cheap for a dinner party, 'half price it is today.'

'What meat is it?' the mince looked strangely pale.

'It's a mixture,' he said. 'Make a lovely Shepherds pie. A couple of Oxo's and Bob's your uncle.'

'My oven doesn't work,' she said.

'Her oven doesn't work,' the butcher shouted to his assistant chining meat in the cold room. 'Any suggestions Ron?'

Ron regarded the mince the butcher had weighed out. 'Meat balls,' he pronounced after some thought. 'In a tomato sauce, here'ya.' He placed a tin of tomatoes on the counter and then robbed the window display of a bunch of parsley.

'Plenty of pepper, you can't go wrong.'

In the market Leila bought a packet each of red and black pepper and a packet of rice. And that was nearly all her money. She would have liked to make a fresh salad, but settled for a cut price dented tin of green beans.

When she unwrapped the meat that evening the smell of it was disturbing. She decided to disguise it with the entire contents of the pepper packets. The addition of the parsley and onion transformed the smell into an appetising fragrance.

Only her brother turned up for the dinner party. His friends were busy, he said.

There had been no word from the nun or Robin. A day later a plain postcard arrived from Mr Boston to say thank you for the invitation but unfortunately it clashed with a previous engagement.

The brother and sister sat on the edge of the bed with plates of meat balls balanced on their knees.

'I wonder how Pup is getting on?' Leila heard herself ask in a voice that sounded like someone at a party attempting to make conversation.

Ben shrugged. 'What happened to your friends?' he asked as if he hadn't heard.

'I don't know,' Leila said, 'And I don't care.'

'Their loss,' Ben said and tipping back a second glass of water.

'Why are you crying?'

'I'm not! It's the pepper.'

'What is it called, this food?'

'Meat balls.'

'What balls?'

'Balls of Fire,' Leila said and laughed. Her tongue was burning. Ben laughed as well. 'My sister the cook,' he said placing his arm around her.

HEAVENLY FLAPJACKS

125 g (5 oz) butter
125 g (5 oz) soft brown sugar
75 g (3 oz) golden syrup
250 g (8 oz) rolled oats
1 teaspoon ground ginger

Melt the butter with the sugar and syrup, and then stir in the rolled oats and ginger. Turn into a greased shallow 20 cm (8 inch) tin and smooth down with a knife.
Bake in a preheated moderate oven at 350F/ 180C/ Gas mark 4 for 25- 30 minutes until golden brown. Cool in the tin for two minutes, and then cut into fingers. When completely cool remove from tin.

The elderly Sibley sisters ran an employment agency in a dark semi- basement close to Victoria Station. Attached to the railings outside were weather-damaged, plastic-covered, hand-lettered offerings and enticements. 'Are you sensible and efficient?'... 'Meet interesting people'... 'Managing director seeks his Girl Friday...'

There was a position with a publishing house, to start immediately.

'Now you're not a student or anything of that sort?' the rounder Sibley sister enquired.

'Miss Biffin is looking for a permanent girl.'

'A permanent reliable girl,' the other sister echoed.

The publication in question was a railway directory listing world-wide track, gauges and rolling stock from the upper Andes to the outer reaches of Jaipur. The offices occupied two rooms on the third floor of a commercial tower block. The editor was the elusive elfin-like Mr Marcus Montague, whom Leila encountered in her second week there.

'You're new,' he declared as if it were some guessing game.

At the time she was laying out his tea tray in the office pantry, one of her scheduled tasks. He had popped his head round soon after his return from lunch to enquire if tea could be a little earlier today.

'Terrible thirst, blame the fish,' he said. 'They will over-season the fish.'

The honour of taking the tea tray into the Editor's office presently belonged to the sturdy middle-aged Miss Biffin, the assistant editor, as she liked to be known. It was a subject of constant rivalry between herself and the only other employee, a bespectacled young shorthand typist/secretary called Doreen.

From her desk behind the door Leila pondered on Doreen's irreproachable attributes. She was of normal height, normal colouring, every detail correct, from the polished pearly finger nails to the modest dab of face powder on her pale face - as if assembled according to a theoretical list of requirements titled, 'The model secretary.'

She reminded Leila of a bakery shop window display she passed daily on her way home when she was at school. On a bed of sun faded pearl grey satin yardage sat a dusty three tiered miniature classical pillared occasion cake. 'Made to Order,' it said. Leila had heard a mother scoff at a child, 'Of course it isn't real you sillybilly. Its cardboard covered in icing. Otherwise it would go mouldy.'

She soon learnt why she had been recruited. It was clearly not for the work. It was to give Miss Biffin status. Not only did the two women compete over the taking in of the tea tray, they vied to answer the telephone and to control the post book. Miss Biffin's mother was an amateur philatelist and until Doreen's arrival in the office Miss Biffin had unchallenged rights on all stamps entering her domain.

Uncontested duties were the tearing off of the morning calendar page; the setting out of the tea tray and the writing in and gumming up of received new mileages into the mock up for the following year's directory.

The process was simple and sticky. Pages were sent out with an invitation to up-date where appropriate. They returned in a variety of type faces and handwriting styles from all over the world in violet, black and green inks. Leila's job was to copy the figures and details of the new entries for Mr Montague's appraisal. These were returned to her for sorting alphabetically. She then filed them in readiness for Miss Biffin to mark up for the printers.

Seldom did more than two or three entries arrive for her to deal with daily. On some days none.

Leila asked Miss Biffin if there was anything else she wanted doing. Miss Biffin closed her eyes in deep irritation.

'There is plenty for you to do, if you will but do it correctly. You might, for instance, try to prevent your glue from smearing.'

'She's always in a bad mood on alternate Tuesdays,' Doreen said. It was Miss Biffin's afternoon for electrolysis.

'D'you want anything done?' Leila asked Doreen.

'No fear! Hard enough to keep going as it is.'

Doreen explained the situation: Miss Biffin had been Mr Montague's assistant for donkey's years. But then the firm expanded and they brought in new people who said editors had to have secretaries with proper qualifications.

'The Biffin can't do shorthand or even type properly. But they couldn't sack her, because she knows the directory back to front. When they brought me in she threw a fit and threatened all manner of things. They pacified her with saying she could have her own assistant, that's you dearie. Anyway, what's your game?'

Leila was startled. 'Nothing!'

'Oh come on, don't tell me you mean to stay.'

'Yes.'

'You're the fifth in two years. She keeps that agency going. Nobody can stand it for long.'

'I'm all right,' Leila said.

'We'll see,' said Doreen. 'We'll see.' Doreen was only sticking the job because she and her fiancé were saving to go to Australia. 'She's tried to edge me out from day one, but I'm up to her tricks.'

The deepest annoyance Doreen was able to lay on Miss Biffin was the time she spent alone with Mr Montague taking dictation. Miss Biffin was bad tempered throughout these daily sessions, reappraising the directory-to-be with faster and faster page turnings. She ordered that the office door be kept open. From her desk she had a full of view of Mr Montague's door. She instructed Leila to enquire whether tea was required.

'They've just had it,' Leila protested.

Miss Biffin repeated the instruction in a voice loaded with rage. 'Kindly do as you are asked.'

On one occasion she sent Leila to knock on the editor's door to enquire if there was any urgent post to go.

'He said, no thank you very much,' she reported back. 'They're doing dictation.'

'Dictation! In the olden days,' Miss Biffin's voice quivered, 'there was no necessity for dictation.'

If a letter was required to be composed all one needed to be told was to make such and such enquires for such and such a purpose, and it was done. 'It does not require dictation and shorthand typing! And what letters could possibly need to be dictated that take fifty minutes!' The pink patches caused by yesterday's electrolysis shone through her pan-cake make up.

'Where is it you're going for your holidays Miss Biffin?' Leila asked to change the subject.

'Pitlochrie,' Miss Biffin brightened for a moment. 'Mother and I always go there. We stay in a small guest house. The flapjacks are out of this world. Mother and I treat ourselves to a chocolate flapjack every afternoon in Pitlochrie.'

'I'm going to Damascus,' Leila said.

'Damascus!' Miss Biffin was unbelieving.

'A friend of mine is living out there. She said I could come any time. She's a Princess so they've got loads of room.'

Miss Biffin seemed to have forgotten her anger and looked amused for the first time all day. 'Well she would have if she's a princess. She'd have a palace wouldn't she?'

'Yes.'

'And no doubt it has its own private rail line to the mountains.'

'I suppose so,' said Leila

'To take you and your princess's friends to her own personal ski resort.'

'I don't ski.'

Miss Biffin suddenly stood. 'Then I suggest you learn'.

PICKLED HERRING WITH SALAD

½ kilo (1 lb) new potatoes
3 pickled herring fillets cut into pieces
125 ml (5 fl oz) fresh soured cream
1 Granny Smith apple, cut into small slices
1 small red onion, sliced
2 hard-boiled eggs, sliced
Grated nutmeg
Cayenne pepper
Salt and black pepper

Boil the potatoes until tender. Remove the skins and slice thickly. Combine the potatoes, herring, apple, onions, nutmeg, salt, black pepper and most of the soured cream. Put in a bowl; lay the egg slices on top. Spoon the last bit of cream over the egg. Sprinkle with cayenne pepper.

To go with the mustard yellow sweater Leila chose a brown skirt. The sweater had shrunk in its first washing and the zip on the skirt was broken. It was part of a discarded suit her German aunt had given her. She would wear them under a woollen turquoise coat she had borrowed from her mother's wardrobe in the hospital. 'What do you want a coat for?' her mother asked. 'It's summer.'

'In case it rains,' Leila said.

'For rain you take a raincoat,' Mrs Adon said. She was in the day room embroidering a tray cloth with chain stitch flowers. Leila did not own a raincoat good enough for an interview. Hers was a navy blue school coat with a frayed buckle and a hem that showed where it had been let down.

She also borrowed her mother's high heeled shoes. They were too tight but she did not plan to walk in them. They would just be for the interview she explained to her mother.

'I won't stretch them,' she promised.

'You are taking my best clothes from me,' her mother was crying. 'I will never see them again.'

'You will, you will,' Leila promised. 'And I'll bring you back a present from Devon.'

'What will you bring me?'

'A surprise,' she promised, 'a nice surprise.'

'I want a pickled herring,' the mother said. 'That's all I want from you.'

Her mother was remembering a herring she had eaten as a child in Amsterdam. It was fished out of an enormous wooden barrel with wooden tongs and served fastidiously on a glass plate accompanied by speckled bread and a plate of green beans.

Leila had returned to the college to discover that she had been expelled for constant absence. Since she had not submitted the required pieces of work for marking it had not been possible to assess her endeavours.

'One did at times wonder the purpose of your enrolment here,' the class tutor said.

'To get an education,' Leila said.

'Aha,' the tutor nodded.

There seemed little point in attending further classes now. She spent the remainder of the day in the college library looking up jobs in the newspapers laid out in the reference section.

There were positions for junior cooks, vegetable cooks, hospital cooks, offices wanted clerks, sensible experienced girls, and shops wanted enthusiastic presentable counter assistants. Garment houses wanted finishers and models.

Under publishing she saw the advertisement for a junior reporter. She bought a notepad and packet of twelve envelopes and twelve stamps

'Dear Sir, I am the girl you want for the job you advertise. See me and decide.' She sent this letter to eleven other job vacancies for which she was supremely unqualified. These included a position with Air France as a trainee ground stewardess; a florist in Mayfair, a beautician in Selfridges, a trainee officer with the Merchant Navy, a Post Office sorter, a children's nurse, secretary at the BBC, a kennel maid at White City.

The only response came within a week from the newspaper in the West Country.

The proprietor, a Mr Austin Nankivell, would meet her at the Exeter Hotel for an informal interview one p.m. prompt. 'I like your spirit!' he had added as a PS to his letter.

The day before the interview Leila waited on the stairs of a school of hairdressing to be selected for free hair styling. 'It's for an interview,' she confided to the Nigerian woman allocated to her. 'I just want to look normal.'

The Nigerian woman patted her into the seat and began cutting. 'Nothing extreme,' Leila was alarmed at the amount of hair the Nigerian was lopping off. 'Don't worry yourself,' was all the Nigerian said as she continued working the hair with clips and comb and scissorings.

Leila stared at her face in the mirror. She looked like a victim of ringworm. She bought a brown beret.

Everyone else on the train was in summer clothing. She felt like a foreigner.

In the sweltering compartment she took off the turquoise coat and folded it inside out before reaching up to stow it on the opposite rack. Her underarms were damp.

Sitting in the compartment was a woman wearing a hand-made green gingham frock with matching bolero. The bronze haired little girl at her side wore a miniature version of the same pattern and her brother sported shorts in the same material.

'We're off to Penzance,' the woman said, 'aren't we children. To stay with Aunty Dorothy and Uncle John in their lovely bungalow by the sea.'

'That's nice.'

'Oh it's ideal for family holidays,' said the woman, 'we always have such lovely times there.'

The smallest child passed Leila a notebook and a pencil. Leila drew a picture of an orange. 'What's that?' she asked the child. The child glanced to its mother for approval and then whispered behind her hand to Leila.

'No,' said Leila. The child guessed again and Leila shook her head again.

'Yes it is!' the child blurted out. 'It's a ball!' The woman pulled the child back on to the seating and asked Leila if she had brothers and sisters.

'No, I'm an orphan,' she said. The woman smiled tightly and told the children they could start on their sandwiches.

Leila turned to the window and closed her eyes. When she woke the woman and the children had left the carriage. Leila's brown beret had slipped from her head on to carriage floor.

As the train approached Exeter she changed out of her brogues into her mother's high heels. The only other person in the carriage now was a rustic looking middle-aged man. He eyed her with disdain as she pulled on her beret and put on her coat.

'You'll roast in that,' he remarked. 'They've had spontaneous fires in the cornfields and there's fire warnings on the moors.'

Leila said: 'I know.'

'You're not from these parts, then,' the man observed as she dabbed her streaming face with a handkerchief.

'No.'

'You don't feel the heat then?' he persevered.

'I like the heat,' she said.

Mr Nankivell was waiting for her on the platform. He spotted her at once.

'You're the London girl,' he said. 'Follow me.'

Pink faced and with thinning blond hair, he reminded her of a toddler in his baggy linen suit and rosy cheeks.

'Come along, come along.' He hurried to a small saloon car and she followed on the toe-breaking shoes as fast as she could. He had booked a table for them at the monolithic Exeter Hotel. Leila urgently needed to use the toilets. She was on the look out for the sign to the Ladies but Mr Nankivell was urging her towards the dining room.

'This way, this way,' his slightly bowed legs sped onwards.

He was obviously a familiar and valued customer. A waiter speedily wended his way towards them at the doors.

'Nice to see you again Sir,' the waiter pulled out chairs.

'Shall I take Madame's coat?' he asked.

'Where's your toilets?' Leila asked.

The attendant in the bathroom surveyed her as she washed her hands. 'There is a cloakroom along the corridor,' she informed Leila. 'Where Madame can leave her outdoor attire.'

'I'm all right'.

On her return Mr Nankivell was studying the menu. The dining room thronged with well to do farming and office types and their wives in cool outfits. The windows had been opened and two fans brought in to boost the two overhead.

Unlike many of the nearby diners Mr Nankivell seemed oblivious to Leila's unseasonable clothing other than to remark, 'You're the Chelsea type, aren't you.'

She read through the menu.

'I normally recommend the roast rib,' Mr Nankivell stated. 'But I'd say it was too hot for roasts, wouldn't you Clarkson?' he addressed the waiter.

'They said the vol au vents were very nice.'

'Not too keen on vol au vents, what about yourself?' Mr Nankivell asked Leila.

'I'll have whatever you're having.'

He was having the fillets of plaice. Leila changed her mind. She would have the pickled herring.

'That's a starter,' Mr Nankivell pointed out.

'I know,' she said.

As they waited for the order he withdrew her brief letter from his jacket pocket.

'This is a rum application,' he said. 'What makes you want to move to the West Country?'

'I'd like a change,' she said.

'What makes you think you can do the job?'

'You can give me a week's trial.'

'A week's trial's no good. Can't tell a thing in a week.'

Her job would be to act as a junior reporter in an office of three.

'I ought to recruit a local lad. Plenty of local lads will jump at the chance you know.'

He seemed set on the idea of a local lad until the arrival of the pudding.

'Then why did I advertise in the national Press, tell me that Miss, if I wanted a local lad, why go to the expense of national advertising?'

He refilled her wine glass. 'Come along, come along, think!'

'You want someone different'.

'Precisely,' she felt a hand squeeze her thigh under the table. 'Precisely, my dear.'

The pickled herring when it arrived was not the brown melting soft salty fillet her mother yearned for. This one had been rolled and skewered and tasted of acid. The flesh was raw and rubbery and the skin had the markings of a snake.

MRS WILDBLOOD'S SANDWICHES

Scrambled Eggs with Smoked Salmon and Dill on Muffins

Serves 2 for breakfast

3 eggs
3 tablespoons milk
25 g (1 oz) butter
Salt and freshly ground black pepper
Smoked salmon scraps
Small handful dill, chopped
2 muffins or buttered bread slices.

Beat together the eggs, milk, salt and pepper. Melt the butter in a saucepan and pour in the egg mixture. Stir for about half a minute and then add the salmon and dill. As soon as the egg starts to thicken take it off the heat and stir. It will continue to cook against the hot sides of the pan. Serve on hot buttered muffins or between thick slices of buttered bread.

A typed letter arrived for Leila from Mr Nankivell with three pieces of information and a request.

She had been successful in obtaining the post of junior reporter, she was to start the following Monday, digs had been arranged at The Laurels with the Wildbloods and would she wear more suitable footwear when on duty. A hand-written PS in black ink at the foot of the page exclaimed, 'I liked your yellow top!'

There was no reason to stay in London. The She-Pole had threatened to throw her out when she complained about rain coming in through the windows. Her father had disappeared and her mother was ill again. Ben seemed evasive when she tried to meet him, Suha had not written and once in the college when she had bumped into Roy he had said something extremely unpleasant. She needed to start again.

The journey from the station to The Laurels was an uphill half hour. Two taxi drivers watched Leila's lopsided progress begin the ascent with the big brown suitcase she had bought in a junk shop. The metal banding and reinforced corner pieces added to its weight.

'You'll not walk it there,' the senior taxi man had advised when she asked for directions.

She would have had sufficient for a taxi had she not spent her last money on a meal on the train. The decision to sit in the diner had been impulsive.

She had ordered the egg salad and immediately regretted it. Stale mayonnaise masked two mounds. When cut through the egg yolks were grey rimmed and the whites rubbery. The lettuce was gritty and the three limp slices of tomato left an aftertaste of mould. The middle-aged waiter proffered a lank roll from a doily-lined basket.

'Bread roll, Madame?' he dropped it on her plate before she had time to reply. 'Something to drink, Madame?' he flashed open the wine list without conviction.

She felt he was sneering at her. She asked for lemonade.

She would have liked to leave him a big tip just to let him know he was wrong about her penury. She left him a crumpled napkin and a half eaten roll.

The terms at The Laurels were half board. Mr Nankivell had settled her first week's payments in advance. As she trudged up the hill past the cake shops, a dispensing chemist, a boutique, a book shop, fishmongers, two butcher's shop, Leila rehearsed several approaches of asking Mr Nankivell for an advance.

The Wildbloods - Gilbert and Audrey and their daughters Alison and Camilla - were taking their tea seated on an assortment of battered garden chairs as she opened the gate and approached along a gravel path.

Mr Wildblood, portly bespectacled and in his middle years, rose to meet her. The small girls ran behind but were instructed by their father to return and finish their tea and did so without argument. Mrs Wildblood stood and smiled ready to greet the new house guest. She was about forty, and dressed like a girl in a home-made dirndl skirt and fawn twin set. Her baby blue eyes were magnified by horned-rimmed glasses and she wore an Alice head band.

A proper family, Leila thought. A normal family.

The house, standing in its own grounds, was substantial, backed by tall swaying birches and hedged with dense privets. There were many rooms, all in need of refurbishment.

The dilapidation, like the Wildbloods, was not hidden or disguised. The integrity would always be there. The china on the tea table was various, cracked and faded but it was Spode. The rugs in the hall were frayed and sun bleached but they were Persian.

The furniture was assorted and in need of re-upholstery and repair but it was not replica.

Leila's room was at the top of the house and in grander days had been the maid's room. It was plain, unadorned and without heating. There was a recently installed hand basin by the window, a small chest of drawers positioned opposite the bed and a faded corner rail curtained in fading green chintz to provide hanging space. A posy of garden flowers in a pottery vase had been placed on the window sill. Mrs Wildblood re-arranged a swooning marigold.

'It's a small room I know and we can try and find you a table of some sort to work on should you need it.'

'It's nice,' Leila said. 'I like it.'

Mr Wildblood placed Leila's case at the foot of the bed. 'I'll make a fresh pot of tea,' he volunteered.

'Thank you darling,' his wife said. 'We'll be down in a tick.'

She showed Leila the bathroom along the passage.

'We thought you might like to take your bath after supper. I'm afraid we're on coal and the boiler only runs to one bath at a time.'

In London Leila had used the municipal baths once a week.

'We do hope you'll be happy here,' Mrs Wildblood said. 'Come down when you're ready for some tea.'

Leila washed her face and looked out of the small window. She could hear Wildblood family voices from below.

'She's from London,' she heard Mr Wildblood inform the children.

'She's got a funny voice,' one of the girls piped out, 'and she sweats.'

'That's quite enough from you Camilla,' Mrs Wildblood sounded irritated.

Laid out on a decorated china plate were three tiny triangles of sandwiches.

'Tomato and this one's scrambled eggs. With chives.'

'Audrey's special. The best sandwich in the world. In my humble opinion,' Mr Wildblood said proudly.

'Gilbert!' Mrs Wildblood reprimanded. 'It's just a simple sandwich

'Only stating the honest truth'.

The two daughters of the house watched intently as Leila bit into the egg sandwich. Unobserved she would have popped the entire triangle into her mouth. Now realising something daintier was expected she slowly bit into a corner of the sandwich and wiped her mouth with the linen napkin provided.

'Smashing,' was her verdict. Mrs Wildblood blushed again.

'We're not allowed to say smashing,' Camilla said, 'Are we daddy?'

'It's good,' Leila added. 'Best I've ever tasted.'

It was also the smallest. In the days to come she was to sit in front of portions so modest she often supplemented them with buns from the cake shop.

'What d'you think of the Wildbloods?' Arthur Willis, the chief sub editor challenged her when she arrived at the office on the Monday.

'Very nice.'

'Not starving you then?'

'No.'

Arthur Willis and Leila disliked each other on sight - Leila for his undisguised misogyny, he for her dubious skills and antecedents and the fact that his detested master Mr Nankivell had chosen her in preference to a couple of able young men he had lined up.

'Last chap they had said she sliced the meat so thin you could see the plate through it.'

'It's very good quality food,' Leila said loyally. 'They're very kind people.'

'He lost his money abroad, you know' Arthur said. 'That's why they take lodgers. He's one of Nancy's church friends. Stick together like treacle.'

Nancy was Arthur's name for Mr Nankivell whom he despised.

'Man's a born idiot,' he'd mutter. 'Wouldn't be anywhere but for family money. And he's frittered most of that away on his hare - brained schemes.'

Mr Nankivell called Leila into his office on her first morning.

'Settling down all right?' he asked.

Arthur had given her a pile of filled in wedding forms to convert into copy for the marriages page.

Name of bride, of bridegroom, service conducted by, ceremony held at, hymns chosen, the bride was given away by, the bride wore, with a bouquet of, a head-dress of, the gown was made by, the bridesmaids were, they wore, the best man was...honeymoon will be a week in the Isle of Wight; touring the Black Forest, sailing in the

Greek Islands, climbing in the Alps, a secret destination. Photographs accompanied the forms, girls of all description, plump ones, old ones, happy ones, serious ones, in a variety of dresses and bouquets....lily of the valley, pink carnations, freesias, tea roses,

The going-away outfits were café au lait ensembles, lemon two-piece with matching coat, aubergine coat with cream accessories, light chocolate woollen suit, ivory blouse.

'I'm getting used to it,' Leila said.

'Digs all right?'

'Very nice.'

'Jolly good.'

'You're not a virgin are you?'

'What's it got to do with you?'

Mr Nankivell looked startled. 'No need to take offence. Perfectly simple observation. Modern London woman and all that.'

He clapped his hands. 'I like your spirit,' he said. 'I think I might stand you lunch. What about it? Eh?'

The Red Dragon Inn dining room was the town's meeting venue for the Rotary Club. Situated opposite the law courts it was also patronised by jobbing lawyers and local solicitors. Mr Nankivell introduced her to men in tweeds and grey suits.

'My new recruit,' he smiled, 'all the way from London.'

She had a feeling they were sneering.

'All the way from London, eh, did you catch that Melvyn, Austin's importing girls from London now.'

Mr Nankivell had booked a table in the upstairs carvery. 'Eat as much as you like, best roast beef in the county.'

'Eat up, eat up,' he urged, 'I want to show you something of the area.'

He drove them in his cream saloon at an erratic pace through small villages, country lanes, working quays, factory sites, past farms and eventually parked in a leafy lay-bye.

'What are we stopping for?' she asked.

'I thought we might enjoy the view.'

They sat silently for a few moments.

'There's a rug in the boot,' he said. She glanced at him; he looked upset, like a child about to burst into tears. 'I won't hurt you.'

'I know you won't.'

After a while she took his freckled hand and patted it. He leaned his balding head on her breast and she stroked it like she had stroked her small brother in the orange grove to put him to sleep. 'I'm quite harmless,' he said. 'But there's no need to advertise it to the world.'

He dropped her off at the top of the road.

'Wildbloods are conservative types. Don't want them getting the wrong idea.'

She opened the car door. 'Mr Nankivell,' she asked as if the notion had only just occurred to her, 'is it possible for me to have an advance on my wages please?'

'I should think so,' he said. 'You're not about to do a flit, are you?'

'No,' she said. 'I like it here.'

THE TREASURE'S PASTIES

For the pastry
400 g plain flour
100 g butter
100 g lard
1 beaten egg

First make your short crust pastry: sift the flour into a large bowl, add a pinch of salt, then rub in the butter and lard with your fingertips. Add 2-3 tablespoons water and make it into a dough. Knead the dough briefly on a floured surface and chill while you make the filling.

For the filling
200 g (7 oz) potato
100 g (4½ oz) parsnip
450 g (1 lb) minced rump steak
1 small onion
freshly ground white pepper, salt
a little chopped parsley
a little white stock.

Roll pastry into rounds the size of tea saucers. In the centre of each pile with an equal mixture of minced rump steak, potato and, parsnip cut into small cubes, finely chopped onion and parsley.

Moisten with clear stock; shake over with white pepper and salt. Brush half the circle with water, bring together with the other half.

Press the edges firmly and flute with your fingers to make a nice edging. Sit up with the fluted edge on top, brush with beaten egg and bake in a hot oven for 15 minutes then lower the heat and cook for a further 30 minutes. Eat hot or cold.

Audrey Wildblood, for all her penury, employed a home help who came in the shape of a slack-jawed thick-set bottle blonde called Daisy Bellows. Daisy worked at The Laurels alternate Fridays, to give the place a seeing to, as she put it.

'Mind you,' she confided to Leila, 'it's only because he was so good with my Bill's knee like.'

Bill was Daisy's husband and while she polished the dining table, jabbing at the missing pieces of inlay with her stubby nails, she divulged how she came to be cleaning for the Wildbloods. Bill worked on the tugs and he'd slipped and twisted his knee.

'That was three years ago now and he still suffers from it. The doctor sent him to the hospital to Mr Wildblood for the physiotherapy. 'Course they only give you the two sessions and then it's up to you to go private if you can afford it which we could not do at that time having just taken out the hp for the washing machine and there was the instalments on the motor bike still outstanding. Mr Wildblood come up to our house with his lamps and gave Bill extra treatment and said he needn't pay until he could afford it. I reckon he needed the practice as well because he was the assistant physio, he'd only just qualified.

'They say he lost his money in the tea plantations and they came back with nothing. The wife's mother's money paid for this house. A bit grand, wouldn't you agree for an assistant at the hospital? It takes some upkeep. And she doesn't work other than her voluntary efforts for the church. And the kiddies' clothes, it's all second hand she gets from the nearly new shop in Market Street and hand me downs from her posh pals. I wouldn't put my kids into second hand no matter what. I'd rather go out scrubbing...'

It was Leila's afternoon off. Later in the evening she was to cover the annual meeting of the local chess club. Mrs Wildblood was out to tea with the children and Leila had the house to herself.

'Daisy does chat,' Mrs Wildblood warned. 'It might be an idea to go for a walk.' Leila was tired out from a morning of trudging to collect whist drive results from premises at both ends of the town. She planned to nap and later, if it was fine, to read in the garden.

As soon as Mrs Wildblood had left Daisy was knocking at her bedroom door.

'I don't want to be disturbing you, but I shall be using the Hoover,' she said, peering into the room.

'So this is where she's put you. It used to be the yellow room she put her visitors in. The little girls are in there now. The yellow room it's got a nice wardrobe and double windows, it's a better room all round. I expect you feel a bit cramped in here.'

'No, I like this room,' Leila said. Daisy said she'd give her a call when she'd made a pot of tea. In about half an hour if that was all right.

'I expect you'd like a bite of something as well. Young people's always ravenous, I know that from my own three. Gannets, the lot of them. And I've heard she doles out small rations. Last but one chappie she took in said she give him half an egg for breakfast and one rasher snipped in two, never more the one slice of bread and no jam ever. Only the thick marmalade, which he could not abide. He left to stop with Mrs Dilkes at the bottleneck. Messy woman with no sense of tidiness whatsoever, but she keeps him full and that's what young men want. They don't want to be going hungry. Many's a time I brought him one of my pasties to keep him stoked up. He was training for the police and that's hefty work. I've a couple of pasties in my bag for my Stephen. He likes a pasty on his way home from school and often as not he'll eat a couple'.

The pasty had been warmed on the Aga. Daisy cut it in two and held the plate up to Leila. 'Take a whiff of that,' she said. It smelt of comfort. It tasted of deep satisfaction.

As an idea for the features page Leila suggested a pasty competition.

'Capital, capital,' Mr Nankivell enthused. The judging by a domestic science teacher, the chairman of the magistrates and the captain of the local football team and Mr Nankivell was done at the W.I hall. There were 41 entries. Daisy's pasty came first. Her prize was dinner for two at the Red Dragon, her picture on the front page and the publication of her recipe in the paper.

RESTORATIVE SOUP

Chicken Soup with Knaidlach
(Otherwise known as Jewish Penicillin)

For the Soup

1 large chicken carcass and 2 packets giblets
1 large onion cut into quarters
2 carrots cut into pieces
1 leek
1 turnip cut into quarters
2 celery stalks and leaves, roughly chopped
2 sprigs parsley
Salt and pepper

For the knaidlach (matzo dumplings)

2 eggs
75 g (3 oz) matzo meal
2 tablespoons finely chopped parsley

In a large pan put the carcass with 1 ¾ litres (3 ½ pints) water. Bring to the boil and remove any scum. Add the vegetables, parsley and salt and pepper. Simmer, covered on a very low heat for 2½ hours, adding water if necessary. Strain the broth and remove the fat. A few minutes before serving add the knaidlach.

To make the knaidlach beat the egg whites until stiff, fold in the lightly beaten egg yolks, then the matzo meal, parsley and salt. Chill for 30 mins. Shape into balls and drop into boiling salted water. Simmer for about 20 minutes.

Not many weeks after Leila had moved into The Laurels a flu epidemic struck the area. Camilla and Alison developed high temperatures and hacking coughs and had to stay in bed. Mr and Mrs Wildblood caught the infection and moved around the house in shabby dressing gowns wet nosed and bleary eyed to top up hot water bottles and make drinks.

Before Leila left the house in the mornings she filled the hod for the Aga with coal from the basement, raked out the dead ashes, opened the downstairs curtains, fed the cats and knocked on the Wildblood bedroom to see if there was any shopping or errands she could do for them. She returned at lunch time with aspirins and lemons and a bottle of Bovril and fresh bread. The Wildbloods were still all feverish in their beds.

'Shall I call the doctor for you?' she asked.

'Goodness no. It's only the wretched flu. But if you could.... fend for yourself it would be a help, I'm really not up to cooking,' Mrs Wildblood could not now complete a sentence without being interrupted by a bout of coughing.

At the office Mr Nankivell was down with it as was Mr Rutgers the advertisement manager and two of the three girls who helped collate and circulate the paper. A retired ex-employee had been contacted to do a stint but he was also ill.

'Looks like it's just you and me to hold the fort,' Arthur Willis said. 'What a treat, eh?'

Up to now his regard for Leila's abilities was blatant contempt.

'You can't do shorthand, you can't spell, you don't drive, you don't know the area. No one in his right mind would have recruited you.'

On sufferance before the epidemic Arthur sent her to collect names of mourners at church doors for the funeral pages, to cover jumble sales, school concerts and venues of no consequence. She wrote up wedding forms and auction prices, W.I meetings, and dog show results which were brought in or sent in by post. On one of the few occasions she was sent out of the office on a story it was to inform Nudge Whitehead, a farmer, he had won £20 on the Premium Bonds with instructions to ask him what he intended to spend the money on.

She ought to have suspected malice when Arthur gave her directions to the farm saying:

'This is your chance to prove yourself.'

After an hour of travelling by country bus through high hedged narrow roads and five-house hamlets she was the last passenger to alight.

'What time d'you go back,' she asked the driver.

'Next Wednesday.' It was a twice a week service. 'There's a taxi service from the garage. I dare say they'll be able to oblige you.'

Arthur's small arrow on his map to the farm from the bus stop proved to be a three-mile walk up a country lane. A cattle lorry overtook her. Leila had to step up a sloping bank to make way for it. Two more vehicles passed and her hopes they might stop and offer her a lift came to nothing. They both sped on.

'Milldole Farm,' was stencilled in faded sea blue lettering on a rotting stake jammed into the ground. It was no longer upright and the rusting gate painted long ago in the same marine colour was difficult to push open.

The afternoon was cold and Leila's back felt the wind as she walked towards farm buildings. Abandoned machinery and a broken cattle trough lined the entrance. Foul puddles and empty sheep pens ran along one side. There was no sign of habitation from the farmhouse other than a grey dog tethered to a kennel who barked as she approached.

The dog continued to bark as Leila knocked on the door. She looked through a window but could see nothing distinguishable through the grimy pane. The barking continued as she stepped over unswept slippery flagstones and knocked on the back door.

The door opened suddenly and an unshaven man in a grubby vest and work trousers stood there. There was an axe in his hand.

'What d'you want?' he growled.

'I'm from the local paper Mr Whitehead,' she said her words running one into the other with fear, 'and I understand you've won a Premium Bond for twenty pounds and wondered if you'd like to tell me what you intend to spend it on.'

The man raised the axe and stepped towards her 'Bugger off,' he said. 'Before I split your head in two

'What did Nudge have to say to you then?' Arthur asked on her return to the office the following day.

She had run back to the road. There was no taxi available at the garage. However, a farm feed rep was there to collect his car and offered to drop her home.

'What are you doing out here anyway?' he asked. When she told him she had been sent to interview Nudge Whitehead he laughed. 'Rather you than me, I won't go near the place. Man's a well known nut case. In and out of loony bins.'

'He wasn't in,' Leila lied to Arthur. 'So there's no story.'

'Pity,' Arthur said. 'I think you might have found him very interesting. Tell you what, as we're so short staffed you can do magistrates court tomorrow. Under age stable girl and the local squire. You do an hour and then I'll nip down from the town hall meeting and take over. There's no one else I can ask. Both my stands-ins are ill and Nancyboy is still bad. There's lineage ordered from the news agencies on both. I can't be in two places at the same time.'

'I think I'm coming down with the flu,' she lied.

'You look all right to me,' Arthur protested.

'I don't feel all right.'

On her way home she stopped at the butchers and asked for chicken's feet.

'We don't do anything like that,' the butcher said with an expression of slight alarm. He had some carcasses and wing tips, if that was any good. In the greengrocers she bought carrots and parsnips, parsley and celery. There was no garlic. No call for it.

Leila found Mrs Wildblood shivering in the kitchen as she waited for a kettle to boil to make the children hot drinks.

Daisy Bellows had promised to call in with some provisions and do some urgent washing but had not yet done so. The vicar's wife was due to visit later.

'Kind of her but quite honestly I can't face visitors at the moment. Oh and the postman left a parcel for you. It's at the foot of the stairs.'

'You go back to bed,' Leila said. 'I'll look after things.'

'But don't you have to return to work?'

'I've got some days off.'

She prepared the vegetables, washed the chicken carcasses and put them all on to simmer.

The brown parcel in the dining room was from Ben. It contained a late birthday present, a book called 'Thus Said Zarathusa' in which he had written, 'To My Sister, the cook and schemer.'

The soup Leila made that day became famous locally. It was widely circulated by Mrs Wildblood to neighbours, friends and associates as A Truly Restorative Soup, for within 24 hours of taking it the Wildblood flu symptoms miraculously subsided to be followed by an almost full recovery within the next few days.

WILD STRAWBERRY PANCAKES

Pancakes with Wild Strawberry Butter

Serves 4

Pancakes
115 g (4 oz) whole-wheat flour
Salt
1 egg lightly beaten
200 ml (7 fl oz) milk
50 ml (2 fl oz) water
1 tablespoon vegetable oil
1 tablespoon kirsch

Wild Strawberry Butter
115 g (4 oz) softened butter
85 g (3 ½ oz) icing sugar
The zest and juice of half a lemon, finely grated
1 - 2 tablespoons kirsch
225 g (9 oz) wild strawberries

Sift the flour and salt into a bowl. Make a well in the centre and add the egg. Beat some of the flour into the egg and then gradually add the combined milk and water. Beat until smooth. Add the vegetable oil and kirsch and leave for 30 mins.

Lightly oil a small heavy frying pan. When it is very hot pour in about 2 tablespoons of the batter and turn the pan so that it is evenly coated. When the batter has set, flip it over with a palette knife and cook for a minute. Transfer to a plate and cook the remainder of the mixture in the same way. Chill the pancakes until needed.

Wash and dry the strawberries. In a food processor (or by hand) cream together the butter, sugar, lemon zest and then add the strawberries, the lemon juice, and kirsch.
Spread the butter over half of each pancake. Fold into quarters and arrange in a heatproof dish and grill for a few minutes until they are bubbling hot.

Out of the blue Ben telephoned Leila at the office. One of the student's parents had a beach cottage not far away on Saunten Sands. A crowd of them were coming down.

'Why don't you visit us?' he suggested. Leila had not heard from him for months. He sounded different. More educated.

She asked Arthur for the week-end off. 'Not up to me, take it up with Nancy.'

Mr Nankivell was seldom in the office. Leila tracked him down at a Rotary function.

'Oh it's you,' he said with an expression of utter surprise, 'shaping up all right?' He made no fuss about her request for time off.

'Just mention it to Arthur, etiquette you know. Where is it you say?' He knew the area, had played golf there, decent enough course.

'How are you getting there?'

His Rotary colleagues were now filling the bar.

'I'll take you if you like. Pick you up outside the office.'

'Anybody can get anything out of that fool by grovelling up to him,' Arthur Willis was his ungracious self.

Leila standing at his desk looked down at Arthur's balding head. There was always a film of fine perspiration on his brow. She waited a moment until Mr Rutgers with a fat man's gracefulness was out of the room.

'I'm fed up with your nastiness,' she said to Arthur. 'I'm leaving.'

She expected him to be pleased. He looked uneasy

'Up to you.'

'No, it's up to you,' she was upset. 'You never stop baiting me. I'm going to speak to Mr Nankivell about it.'

Arthur eased back his chair, stood up and pushed past her and fell forward his chest hitting the desk before he slumped to the ground. The crash brought Mr Rutgers rushing into the room. He knelt beside Arthur and lifted him up.

'You're all right boy,' he said. 'You're all right.'

'Make him a sweet cup of tea quick as you can,' he ordered 'He's having a hypo that's all.'

Arthur's daughter, who worked in the council offices nearby, was fetched to drive her father home. She looked as bad tempered as her father.

'Bloody nuisance he is,' she said, 'I wonder what's brought it on this time.'

Mrs Wildblood insisted on lending Leila a rucksack and a waterproof hat and jacket for her excursion to Saunten. Camilla pressed a toy compass into her hand.

Leila waited outside the office for three quarters of an hour before she realised that Mr Nankivell had forgotten to pick her up. Arthur was now recovered and back at work. She could not face him knowing she had been let down. She picked up her rucksack and headed for the bus station.

There was no direct bus to the dunes. There was a coach, a bus official looked it up, could drop her off seven, ten miles in the right direction, but that was not until tomorrow. Only coach out this morning was an excursion going to the other side of the dunes. Otherwise it was a question of a taxi or private hire. And they could be pricey.

The thought of returning to The Laurels was depressing. She could already hear Camilla's piercing voice: 'But Mummy why is she back already!'

Leila decided to board the excursion coach. A group of hikers were already loading their packs into the underside. She added her small rucksack to theirs. The coach arrived at the dunes just after mid-day. The hikers were a group of Swedes holidaying in the area.

They possessed maps and packets of raisins and sketch pads. 'We are an art group,' a woman in a headscarf explained. 'Every year we go somewhere different to make our drawing and painting.' Leila tramped between the scattered holiday homes on the sands until she found the address Ben had sent. The holiday bungalow was called Jolly's. Evening primroses grew in clumps around it and rabbits scattered as she approached the door. The house was boarded up and locked. Leila sat on the porch and emptied her shoes of sand. The Swedish hikers were passing. They waved and she waved back.

'Nobody in?' their leader, a middle-aged man with a gargoyle grin, guessed.

'Don't be lonely, come with us,' one of the woman insisted.

The group found shelter between the dunes. Two of the men made tea with a picnic kettle and passed round crisp breads and slices of cheese. Then one of the women undressed completely and lay on a rug while the others sketched. 'You don't like to draw?' Leila was asked.

'I prefer cooking,' Leila said.

She went for a walk and discovered tiny wild strawberries growing in profusion. There were cries of delight when she returned with a hatful of them. The art was abandoned for strawberry picking.

At dusk Leila accompanied the Swedes to a caravan site where she helped the girl who had posed naked to make pancakes with the strawberries.

CIDER APPLE PORK

1 kg (2 lbs) belly pork
1 teaspoon ground cinnamon
1 teaspoon ground clove
1 teaspoon ground black pepper
1 dried red chilli, crumbled
1 heaped tablespoon honey
200 ml (7 fl oz) soy sauce
100 ml (3 ½ fl oz) sweet cider
6 garlic cloves
3 cm (1 ¼ inch) fresh ginger

Mix together the chilli and spices and press into the sides of the pork. Put the pork in a plastic bag in a bowl; mix together the remaining marinade ingredients pour over the meat and leave in the fridge overnight.

Place the pork, marinade and 1.25 litres (2 ½ pints) of water in a shallow roasting dish. Bring to the boil, cover with foil and bake in the oven at 300F/ 150C / Gas mark 4 for 2 ½- 3 hours, turning and basting every thirty minutes. Add more water if the meat starts to dry out. The pork is cooked when it gives no resistance to a sharp knife. Reduce the liquid and spoon the sauce over the meat.

The reporters on the opposition newspapers she came across generally regarded Leila as one of Mr Nankivell's many follies. As the first female reporter in the county she came into the same category as the Boxing Day boat race to Lundy Island in which four people drowned; the two year old horse he bought which fell and had to be shot on its first outing; the county wide 'Beauty and Brains' contest abandoned when no finalist ugly or beautiful, was able to correctly answer a single one of Mr Nankivell's exasperating questions (How many legs has an earthworm, the name of God in Czech, Catalan and High German; How long is a moment?)

Harry Hartford was the coming man on the county daily paper. He was twenty one, tall and pretty for a boy, an all round sportsman and whether admitted to or not was lusted after by the majority of the sexually active women of the town and a number who were not.

Arthur was sending Leila to cover the opening of a new sports ground. 'We'll want all the speeches. If you get stuck Harry Hartford will give you a hand and a bit more beside given half a chance,' Arthur sniggered.

Leila had already met Harry in the Press tent at a cattle show. He was among a group of men at a fold-up table drinking from pint glasses and typing and writing out results. The bus had been late and she had missed the early judging classes. She looked around the tent for an unoccupied space. Most of the benches were covered in papers.

'Come and sit here,' Harry called tapping the table.' Shift up everybody,' he called as he made space for Leila. She was reluctant to take up the offer before establishing how she could catch up.

'Does anyone know where I can get the results?' she asked the gathering.

Harry moved along the bench.

'Squeeze in,' he passed her his tray of copy. 'Just change the intro.'

He possessed a portable typewriter. It was going to be easy.

'It's very kind of you.'

He touched her hand. 'Quid pro quo, you'd do me a favour wouldn't you?'

One of the other journalists laughed. 'He never stops does he?'

A girl with beautiful brown eyes dressed in a hound's-tooth check two piece and carrying a shooting stick entered the tent.

'Harry you're not flirting again!'

'No my love, not really,' he winked.' The two went off together.

The other journalists bantered among themselves as they tapped and scribbled out the endless lists of result. 'He'll break her heart before the weekend,' a portly gingery man inserted a new page into his typewriter.

'That was broke years ago, back of the old school playing fields. I can vouch for that. Tasty little pasty.'

A nudge reminded him there was a female listener.

He turned to Leila. 'Getting on all right?'

She nodded.

'Arthur giving you gyp?'

'He doesn't bother me,' she replied.

'He's not a well man. Diabetes.'

'And how's Mr Nankivell? Has he bought any new fillies yet?'

'I don't know what you mean.'

'Leave the girl be Derek,' the portly man called over.'

'Go and taunt someone your own size.'

Leila was already seated at the Press table in the new sports hall scribbling away when Harry slipped in next to her. 'Anything happening yet?'

'Introductions.' He watched her trying to get it all down and then leaned over to whisper into her hair.

'You don't need all this guff. Wait for the speeches.'

She glanced at him. Harry Hartford was a masculine specimen at his peak, radiating optimism and happiness, irresistible, smiling at the world which smiled back to share his delight in life.

'Write when I write,' Harry advised. Leila stopped writing, drew a big butterfly on the open page of her notebook and filled the wings with squiggles.

She felt Harry's leg pressed against hers as he now began to take down the speeches in shorthand. Her pen moved automatically along the lines of her notebook but her attention was on the boy beside her. He stopped writing and passed across his notebook. She stopped writing and read the message he had written in a surprisingly elegant hand: 'Shall we make love?'

She considered the words and not knowing how to respond thought up a line.

'Don't be silly!' she wrote and with a smile slid his notebook back, expecting the note passing to continue.

Almost immediately Harry moved along the bench so that there was now no contact between them. When she turned to look at him she realised she had done the wrong thing. Harry's expression was distant, his eyes cold.

'Can I check some of the names,' she asked as the meeting came to a close.

'Sorry,' he said, 'I'm pushed for time.'

Afraid of not being able to decipher her frantic handwriting of uncompleted words and missed sentences Leila let herself into the office while her memory of the meeting was still fresh. The office cat met her on the dark stairway and watched her two finger typing efforts. 'At the opening of the new sports grounds on Monday ...I did something stupid,' she wanted to write, 'I spoilt my chances...' Chances for what? She knew about falling in love from the cinema and books, from Suha, from the girls at the cigarette factory. It had not happened to her before, the feeling of arousal when Harry touched her.

Ordering what she could make out from her notes and recollection into a coherent report was giving her a headache. Scrunched up pages in the waste paper basket under her desk betrayed her struggle. She was cold and tired and her eyes ached. She realised she would have to reduce the report to a couple of paragraphs and endure Arthur's scathing remarks.

The telephone on Arthur's desk rang.

'How are you getting on?'

'Who's that?' Leila did not recognise the voice.

'Who do you think?'

It was Harry. Driving home he had seen the light in the office and guessed it was her.

'Do you want some help?'

She let him into the office with a feeling of fear and excitement. Harry had worked for the paper as a junior. He knew his way about.

'Shift over,' he said. His breath smelt of beer.

She stood aside as he occupied her chair, read her report, smiled, fisted it into a ball and inserted a new piece of copy paper into the typewriter and began to type, his fingers flying over the keys.

'Make us a cup of tea,' he asked without looking up. 'Two sugars

The kettle and tea making things was kept in the collating room next to a small sink. By the time the tea was made Harry had completed writing up the report.

'Don't I get a thank you?'

'Thank you ,' Leila said.

'You're not going to be mean to me again?'

She shook her head.

'We're on then!' Harry took her hand. 'This is going to be magic.'

There was a settee in Mr Nankivell's room and Harry knew where the key was kept. Leila watched him stretch to reach for it above the door and suddenly decided she didn't want to enter the room.

'No one will know. Promise you.'

His familiarity with the room, throwing the settee cushions on the floor, turning on the desk lamp, the careful way he draped his jacket on the back of Mr Nankivell's chair made her resolute. 'No,' she said.

'You know you want to.' It was a line she'd heard half a dozen times in the cinemas of London.

The thought of being another of Harry's conquests in that room and in all probability the least successful of them decided it.

'Who do you think I am' she pushed him away.

This time her scorn seemed to make him gentler, keener.

'All right, all right,' he said. 'There's no need to get upset.'

Harry's car was a small saloon Ford. 'I'll take you home,' he said. He knew where she lived. In his days as a junior reporter he picked up tennis club results from Gilbert Wildblood.

'Nice chap,' he said. 'And she's a poppet,' and then spoilt it by adding. 'Are you getting enough to eat there?'

'Plenty!'

'You've got a temper!'

'I haven't.'

'I like temperamental girls.'

'You like all girls from what I've heard.'

He laughed. 'Who's been gossiping? It's true I do like women. And they generally like me.'

'You're a big head.'

'Whatever you say.'

He parked the car outside the gates and offered her a cigarette. She could have said no thanks I don't smoke, like they did in the films. And then she could have said, 'I've got to go in now.' She took the cigarette and waited for him to light it. And then she kissed him on the cheek.

'I can't make you out,' Harry said. 'Are we going to make love or not?'

'Can we be friends?'

'Nothing to stop us being friends as well.' They sat smoking. Harry glanced at his watch.

'Have you had your supper?'

Mrs Wildblood would have left a cold plate on top of the refrigerator. A slice of meat and pickles, a wedge of cheese and an apple.

'Not yet.'

'I'm famished,' Harry said.

He lived in a self-contained flatlet above a gift shop. He parked the car at the rear of the premises and Leila followed him up a flight of stairs to a cream painted hardboard door. Harry turned the key and flicked the light switch to reveal a rectangular room containing assorted odds and ends of furniture haphazardly arranged on a moulting grey pile carpet.

The kitchen was surprisingly large and well fitted. The fridge contained an opened tin of corned beef, a shrivelled tomato and a triangle of cheese and milk that had gone off.

'I've got some bread,' Harry lifted the squashed remains of a sliced loaf from a drawer. 'Shall we have a sandwich then? There's some pickle somewhere.'

Leila fingered the bread. It was limp. 'I'll make something,' she said.

'Make what?'

'I don't know yet,' she said, searching the cupboards for ingredients

He stood behind her and held her by the waist. 'And after,' he said, 'You'll be nice with me.'

She moved away.

'Have you got any onions?'

'I'll go and change the sheets,' he said.

By the time Harry returned Leila was stirring a corned beef stew in which floated bread dumplings, the contents of a tin of pineapple, and the tomato. Harry bent over the pot and sniffed.

'What's that?' he asked.

She offered him a spoonful to taste. 'Try it,'

He backed away.

'I can't eat foreign food,' he said.

'It's not foreign,' she protested. 'I made it up!'

'You eat it then'

'I can't,' she confessed. It was too sweet.

They searched the shelves for something else to eat. There was a tin of peas and some stale shortbread biscuits.

'Let's see what Mum has on offer.'

He started the car and they headed inland. A band of fog now draped the roofs of the town like a veil. It was difficult to see the road ahead clearly.

Leila would not have been surprised if Harry had used the fog as an excuse to stop in a lay-by. In a strange way she would have welcomed it. If anything was going to happen between them it would have be somewhere anonymous, secretive and in the night like a dream that could be forgotten. They passed a lay-by. He did not slow down. The visibility was so poor it was only the sound of a hedge scraping the car metal work that alerted Harry he was almost off the road.

'It's getting worse,' Leila peered ahead for road signs.

'Not far now,' Harry did not seem concerned. 'This car knows its way home.'

She was invited into the kitchen by an arthritic white haired large elderly woman, her legs so inlaid with fat her shoes had been slit to accommodate swollen feet.

'She's a nice one. Different anyway,' Mrs Hartford addressed Harry, ignoring Leila throughout. 'Going in for the exotics now are we?'

With near slow motion she opened larder doors, set out plates, sawed bread from an enamel bread bin, stooped dangerously to fetch out a quivering casserole dish from the innards of the range.

'Get that inside you my lovely,' she smiled at Harry. 'Mind you cut it fine for the girl. Girls don't like big chunks.' Leila had never tasted anything like it before. The meat had a deep intensity, the gravy a strange sweetness. 'It's been slow cooked,' Mrs Hartford addressed Harry but the information was obviously intended for Leila, 'with my own cider apples. '

'It's very tasty,' Leila said but Mrs Hartford seemed not to have heard.

'What d'you say Harry? Have I made it up right for you? I know you don't like it too greasy.'

'It's tip top,' Harry said, 'Just the job.'

'I had a notion you'd be wanting something hot.'

She watched them eat with a mother's pleasure all the while conducting a staggered conversation with Harry.

'Been busy boy?' she asked.

'Busy enough.'

'She's not one I've seen before,' she said referring to Leila. 'You do pick them.'

'Any pud?' Harry asked.

'There's always pud for my boy.'

She swayed to the pantry and returned with a half cut apple pie. 'And there's cream if you want it. Leave the dishes to soak,' she instructed before heaving herself up in readiness for bed. 'Night night boy.' They heard her clomp up the stairs.

Mrs Hartford turned out to be Harry's grandmother. He told her this as they faced the open range. He sat on the floor leaning against Leila playing with the hem of her skirt. The sexiness seemed to have gone out of him. Instead there was openness, a soft sadness as he told her about his mother. 'She was a lively girl, so the story goes, an only child, who had it off with a number of local lads.'

His fingering the hem of her skirt reminded her of something long ago connected with her small brother.

Harry went on: 'When she found she was in the pudding club she couldn't say specifically who was responsible. Her mum and dad offered to take the baby in at birth.'

'Where's your mother now?' Leila asked.

'In an institution,' Harry said.

So is mine, she wanted to say. Instead she moved closer to him.

Shortly afterwards Leila left the paper. Different reasons were speculated.

The Wildbloods persuaded themselves it was something to do with the reception they had given her after she stayed out. But it couldn't be helped. There were unwritten house rules and really in the long run it was for her protection. They had left the front door unbolted until eleven thirty but sleep was difficult as they waited for the sound of the door. It was Camilla, lifting the cat out of the kitchen into the hall who alerted her parents to Leila's return at dawn. Mr Wildblood, not yet fully dressed unbolted the front door. Camilla and Alison peered from behind their daddy's dressing gown.

'I stayed with some friends,' she offered as an excuse. 'Sorry I couldn't let you know. It was out in the country and they didn't have a phone.'

Mrs Wildblood entered the hall to order the girls to their breakfast.

'Good morning,' she said icily to Leila and then addressed her daughters. 'Come on you two, I've poured the porridge.'

Normally Leila would have joined the Wildbloods for breakfast but Mrs Wildblood had firmly closed the kitchen door.

Leila went to her room and washed in cold water and changed her clothes. The family were still at breakfast as she slipped out of the house to the office.

Arthur was already in subbing the copy Harry had written up for her.

'Enjoy it, did you?' he asked.

'Enjoy what?' she snapped. She felt aggressive, not in the mood for his jibes.

'The opening, what did you think I meant?'

There was a stack of forms in the wire tray on her desk for her to write up. Births, marriages, deaths. She was becoming quite fast at converting them into the paper's archaic house style. She began typing. Mrs Emily Saunders lately of North Street died in her sleep aged 82 on Wednesday last after a short illness. She is succeeded by her husband Mr George Saunders, her daughters Helen and Margaret and son Trevor, her grandchildren Peter, Simon, Geraldine and Susan, her great grand-daughter Paulette. The funeral will take place at...the funeral arrangements are by...

Arthur glanced across at Leila. She had stopped typing.

'Having some problems?' he asked after a while.

'No,' she said and began typing again. 'The engagement is announced between Miss Stephanie Louise Stanton-Brown, only daughter of Major J.D Stanton-Brown and Mrs Stanton-Brown of Becks House to well known local journalist Mr Henry (Harry) Hartford...'

She left a week before the wedding form came in accompanied by a photograph of the happy bride and bridegroom, a matron of honour, three bridesmaids and a pageboy.

SWEETBREADS À LA ANDRÉ

Braised Sweetbreads
A classic recipe in which the cook uses creative judgement as to amounts.
Lamb or calf sweetbreads
Onion
Carrot
Celery
Fresh herbs
Sherry
Stock

Prepare the sweetbreads as follows: soak in cold salted water for 30 mins - 4 hours, changing the water, whenever it becomes pink from the blood. Place in a saucepan, bring to the boil and simmer for two minutes. Drain and rinse well. Peel off the thin membrane and any tubes. Place a weight on top of them for thirty minutes to create a firmer texture.

Now braise in the oven with the stock, sherry, vegetables and herbs for 45 minutes at 400F/ 200C/ Gas mark 6 until tender.

The next Englishman for whom Leila cooked a meal was called Frank. She had seen an advertisement for an experienced junior reporter on an Essex paper. The post was in their new town branch where Londoners displaced by slum clearance were offered new cleaner lives in a rural setting. It had attracted the young marrieds and aspiring but within a decade had become a different sort of slum - a slum of the culturally rootless.

Leila found the staff on the paper like the goods in the shops, adequate and strangely depressing. Paul Graham, the cigar-smoking editor, had little to say to anyone on the reporting staff. His communication to them was through the chief sub Michael Jefferson, a frail stooping Scotsman on the point of retirement and desirous of a quiet life. The two senior reporters were Angela Graham, the editor's wife, a smart part-timer, always in a dash, and Gerry Mott, a red headed burly Lancastrian, who traded lewd jokes on the phone with his contacts all the while eyeing Leila at her desk opposite his. She dealt with it by moving her desk and chair so that it now faced the sports desk. This was occupied by John Latter, the sports editor, an ex games teacher whose violent temper was responsible for the cracked window and two disabled telephones.

'You want to take up a sport,' he advised Leila shortly after her arrival. 'You're the type who soon runs to fat.'

'I walk,' she said, 'for miles.' One of her tasks was to call regularly on the six Church of England, two Catholic, one Plymouth Brethren, one Methodist, one Jehovah Witness and two Mormons who had set up in the new town. The Mormons were two well-groomed young men with North American accents wearing neat suits.

'Any news?' she asked monotonously each week. 'Not yet a while,' was the usual smiley answer. 'Any converts?'

They operated from a four bedroomed house with a plot at the back designated for a church. In two years they had not managed to recruit a single follower. Leila had interviewed a group of teenage girls who hung about the plot after school and in the holidays. 'Are any of you considering becoming Mormons?'

They giggled behind their hands. 'Seriously,' she pressed them. 'You must be attracted by something, you keep hanging about here.' It was the accents, the girls confessed; they loved listening to the American accents. Next best thing to going to the pictures. Her feature ended on Michael Jefferson's tray. He read it slowly and spiked it.

'What we're after here is hard news,' he said kindly when she asked if he liked it.

Frank Hinds, a harassed 25 year old, was the Corporation's housing department's junior public relations man. Leila had been sent to interview him with a list of complaints from householders.

He answered her questions in a dull ping-pong monotone - 'we are looking into that one, we have that matter in hand, we are expecting a report shortly...our primary concern as always is with the well being of the community...'. Leila countered with a repetitive hand gesture and raised eyebrow that was intended to say 'Boring, boring, boring.'

Frank suddenly sprang up. A sudden migraine. 'D'you mind if we continue this another time?'

She was tapping out the report when the phone on her desk buzzed.

'Council, for you,' Joyce the receptionist sing-songed.

It was Frank. Sorry about cutting the interview. He had recovered now.

'Doesn't matter,' Leila said. 'I've got all I need.'

There was a pause. She could hear his breath. 'Could we meet?'

'What for?' and before he could answer added, 'All right, where?'

She was hoping for a tip off. In her two months on the paper she had not found a single front page item. Her efforts to dredge something of interest from her visits to vicars, youth club leaders, schools and shopkeepers, were subbed down to a couple of paragraphs on the inside pages.

Leila met Frank in the steamy bus terminal cafe. The tables were mostly taken up by tight-faced housewives with pushchairs and teething toddlers waiting for a bus to take them away for a day. Visiting their mums, their old neighbours, an excursion to the sales, anything to escape the sterility of their new lives for a while.

'What will you have?' Frank was waiting on a stool facing the street. The condensation dribbled down the windows.

He returned from the counter with two Colas. He seemed to be trembling as he set down the bottles and handed her a straw.

'How did you know?' he asked in a quiet resigned voice.

'Know what?'

'Please don't talk about it to everyone.'

'What?'

'D'you fancy a walk?'

'A walk?' The vicious winter winds lost in the new town streets got you in the back.

'Please.' He seemed desperate. Leila's imagination leapt to journalistic scoops. What did this boy with his amber eyes and waxy skin imagine she knew?

'Do you think anyone else knows?'

They were heading towards a damp bench on the sodden playing fields.

'You haven't spoken to anyone?'

'About what!' she was becoming exasperated.

Frank replicated the floppy hand gesture she had made at their first meeting.

'Was it my voice?'

Still puzzled, she waited for him to continue. Perhaps it now occurred to him that this girl who had seemed so assured and confident at their meeting was naive. 'I'm queer.'

'Queer?'

'A homosexual. I need to know what gave me away.'

She tried to assure him she had no idea he was a homosexual. She did not think she had ever met one. She had heard of them. She tried to sound objective. In the college library she had picked up a book by André Gide.

'André who?'

A Frenchman who wrote about homosexual flies, to prove that homosexuality was normal in the natural world.

Frank asked her to promise not to discuss his secret with anyone. All he wanted was to seem normal.

'I've got to go,' Leila said. She was now so cold her teeth ached.

'Have you got someone,' he asked as they walked back to the precinct. 'A boyfriend?'

She hadn't.

'Will you go out with me?' To allay suspicion, so he would appear normal. She wasn't sure she liked him.

'Where to?'

'You could ask me to dinner.'

'Alone?'

'That would be rather pointless.'

'Ask John Lattimer and his Mrs.'

'I don't know them,' she protested.

'Here's your chance I'll bring the wine.'

She did not have suitable furniture. In fact she did not yet have any furniture other than a cooker and built-in cupboards. She had been allocated a corporation apartment designed for single occupation, a cheaply built unfurnished one bedroom flat with ill fitting doors, warped skirting boards and a brittle Marley floor tiles so badly laid they cracked with little provocation and showed up every mark. The only way they looked good was with a daily liquid wax polishing.

She had asked for an advance on her wages and with it had bought a fold up bed advertised in the paper, blankets, a kettle, a saucepan and some second hand crockery. She had stuck newspapers on the windows.

'I'm still decorating,' she told Frank the first time he came to her flat.

'Blimey,' he said, 'Where's your furniture?'

Frank was in digs with Edna Marber, a motherly divorcee, who, according to Frank, served him a series of appalling meals - watery mashed potatoes, tinned vegetables and ready-cooked meat she bought from the butcher. Her puddings were custard with everything, mostly tinned fruit, slippery sliced peaches being her favourite.

'On my birthday,' Frank reminisced, as he paced the empty sitting room, 'she threw in some sliced banana.'

During the next couple of weeks they met up to go to the cinema and to collect a flecked yellow plastic topped kitchen table and four metal legged chairs from Miss Marber's shed. She also had some unlined faded floral curtains and a brown ceramic tiled coffee table Leila girl could have. Frank had persuaded Miss Marber to sort through her kitchen cupboards and delivered an assorted boxful of battered saucepans, a colander and metal jug to Leila's door. Leila gave Frank a key to her flat. It was somewhere for him to go when his landlady had her family over, somewhere for a change of scenery.

'What's it in aid of?' John Lattimer asked when Leila invited him and his wife for a meal. 'Nothing in particular,' she said. He was already preparing excuses. He would have a word with his wife, not always easy to book a baby sitter. 'Who else is coming?' She was deliberately vague. One or two people, she mentioned Frank.

'That pansy!' John Lattimer said. 'What d'you want him for?'

Leila told Frank she had changed her mind about a dinner party. However, she would cook him a meal as a thank you for helping her to furnish the flat.

'What do you like to eat?' she asked.

'Surprise me,' he said.

On her day off Leila travelled to London by bus and visited the college. She returned with a recipe copied from an ancient book in the reference library and a carrier bag full of ingredients.

'What's it called? Frank asked as they sat opposite each other, a candle stuck in a bottle lighting the table.

'Sweetbreads à la André Gide,' she replied.

SWEETEST SHISH KEBABS

Moroccan Shish Kebabs

Serves 6
1 kilo (2 lbs) tender lamb

For the marinade
150 ml (5 fl oz) olive oil
2 grated onions
2-3 crushed garlic cloves
1-2 teaspoons cumin
1 teaspoon paprika
2 crushed bay leaves
2 tablespoons mint
Salt and pepper

Remove any fat from the lamb and chop into 2.5 cm (1 inch) chunks. Place in a bag with the marinade ingredients and leave for at least an hour or preferably overnight. Thread the cubes of meat on to flat-bladed skewers (so that they turn easily) and grill for 7-10 minutes turning once. The outside should be browned and the inside pink and juicy.

Leila was sent to cover the opening of a new hospital wing. She was among the group of journalists, councillors, officials and wives led from ward to ward. The pièce de résistance was a plump-cheeked young woman in an iron lung. All that was visible was her smiling face. The woman's hair had been curled into ringlets gripped to each side with primped baby-pink satin ribbon. Her eyelashes were lightly mascara-ed, her lips glossed pretty pink. Fluffy toys dangled in her line of vision.

After writing up this event, which she found under the headline 'Councillors Impressed,' Leila sent a postcard to Ben to suggest they visit their mother together.

They arranged to meet outside Liverpool Street station. There was time to have a coffee before the train left. Leila insisted on getting them.

'My treat,' she said proudly. She reminded herself of her father as she added an expensive slice of chocolate gateau and a portion of apple pie to the tray.

'You choose,' she said. Ben did not want either. The anger she felt at this was also something from her father, the deliberate putting of someone in the wrong. Ben watched her eat both cakes.

'You're getting fat,' he said. It was true. Her clothes were tight on her. She seldom cooked now, filling up on sandwiches and pastries.

'So what,' she replied spooning chocolate into her mouth.

The train was a stopping one. They sat opposite each other in the window seats.

Leila had bought a picnic of sandwiches, chocolate biscuits and orange squash for the journey but now did not feel like offering any of it.

'How are you getting on?' Ben asked.

'What do you mean?'

'Your 'career'.'

'Oh that. I'm applying for other jobs.'

'As what?'

'A ballet dancer, what do you think!' it smarted that he seldom took her seriously.

Leila's life in the new town was a lonely one. Apart from Frank she had not managed to make friends.

Angela Graham, the editor's wife, had invited her to supper. The Graham house was one of the more expensive ranges situated in a private development on the outskirts of the town.

Leila had a bath, washed her hair, changed into an angora navy and white striped skirt and top she had bought from a precinct shop and waited for a bus to take her to the Graham house. She had met Angela briefly a few times in the office and Angela had smiled warmly and said hello.

Angela opened the door dressed in a velvet two piece and gold heeled slippers.

'Come in, came in take your coat off. Gin and tonic, Cinzano...?' the drinks cabinet was open, 'help yourself to a nibble.'

Before Leila had finished her first drink Angela took her for a tour of the house, opening doors and cupboards like an estate agent. 'The bathroom, heated towel rail, dimmer switch' she demonstrated. 'Master bedroom, I insisted on a four-poster, the cover is damask by the way, imported from Italy...Paulie's office, like the cigar cabinet? Controlled humidity....'

The tour ended in the kitchen. 'We had the units made to order. It's American cherry if you're wondering...'. There was a smell of cabbage. 'Cauliflower cheese, Paulie's favourite. Time for a top up, don't you think?'

They had several more top ups as they waited for Paul in between which Angela made several unsuccessful telephone calls to try and locate him.

'Do you mind if I make a personal remark?' Angela leant over Leila, 'You're shedding.'

Her manicured nails pincered stray threads of angora from the settee on which Leila sat. 'Not to worry,' she left the room and returned with a tartan rug for Leila to sit on. 'You didn't mind my mentioning it?'

'Not at all.'

'Another little top up?'

By ten o'clock Leila began to worry about her bus. Angela made another excursion to turn down the cauliflower cheese and two more calls.

'He's got a woman you know. Or why else is he never in, never on time, dodging about, smelling of scent? You don't happen to know who his tart might be.'

Leila shook her head. Angela's voice was bitter. 'And you wouldn't tell me if you did know.'

'I think I'd better catch my bus,' Leila said.

'You catch your bloody bus, go on, you can all sleep with him, I don't care any more.'

Leila could smell burning.

'Shall I turn off your cauliflower cheese?' she asked Angela before she left to run for the last bus.

When she arrived at the office the next day Joyce the receptionist said Mr Graham wanted to see her the minute she came in.

Paul Graham didn't ask her to sit down. 'I've an apology to make to you. Apparently you went home without your supper last night. How did you get on with Angela?'

Leila shrugged. 'Whatever she told you she's got the wrong end of the stick.'

'I know,' she said.

When she saw Frank again she told him he couldn't use her flat any more. The night after Angela's party she had to sleep with the windows wide open. Her flat had smelt of cigar smoke and Frank's scent.

Leila and Ben found their mother in the handicraft room making Christmas cards.

'What have you got me?' she asked eyeing Leila's bag. Leila laid out the salad rolls, fruit and chocolate and half used bottle of scent. Her mother smelt the bottle.

'That's nice,' she said pouring a quantity onto the palm of her hand and rubbing it into the back of her neck.

'And this,' Leila had brought the photograph of the family taken in Trafalgar Square.

'Who's that?' Leila pointed to herself holding her little brother Pup. Her mother didn't respond. 'And that?' Leila pointed to Ben in the picture backing away from the fluttering pigeons. 'It's him, when he was a little boy. Isn't it?'

Mrs Adon snatched the picture from Leila and looked at it closely.

'I know who is that one,' she said. It was of herself. 'She's no good.'

'And him,' she said dabbing at the picture of her husband. 'He should be in a prison.'

'He is in prison,' Ben said.

Leila stared at him.

The last she had heard of her father was a postcard depicting Ely Cathedral care of the college which somehow found its way to the New Town. 'To my dearest daughter,' he had written in biro, 'don't blame your father for things you don't know.'

Why hadn't Ben told her? 'I would have visited him, I could have written to him!'

Ben kept repeating it: 'He asked me not to tell you,' refusing to divulge why Mr Adon had been jailed, how long for or where she could contact him. 'Now shut up about it!'

'But why, just tell me why...' A nurse came over and asked them to keep their voices down.

When they arrived at Waterloo again it was early evening. Leila had stopped nagging, and had retreated into a sulk. Ben had patted her arm and said; 'Don't worry so much' and she had recoiled.

'I'm going to get myself a sandwich,' she said without looking at him and made her way to the refreshment room. He found her facing the window biting into a damp egg and cress sandwich, her eyes loaded with unshed tears.

His voice was soft, beguiling, like a lover's. 'Try to understand...he's only allowed two visits and a couple of letters a month...'.

'Why is it always you? Always you, his favourite!'

'It's not me, you fool.'

'Who are you calling a fool!'

Ben pulled her face roughly towards his. 'It's someone else. He's got someone else now. Another family.'

Leila looked at him uncomprehending. 'He can't,' she said. 'He can't do that.'

'Well he has. He stole some money for them. That's why he's in prison. He didn't want anybody to know.'

'Well I'm going to write to him and tell him what I think,' Leila was recovering.

'Don't,' Ben said, 'be such a bitch.'

They spent the evening in a Turkish Cypriot restaurant.

'Only the sweetest lamb is sacrificed for our kebabs,' the menu announced in broken English.

JUMPING BUCK RAREBIT

Welsh Rarebit with a Kick

Serves 4
50 g (2 oz) butter
1 tablespoon mustard powder
1 dried chilli, crumbled
Salt and pepper
450 g (1 lb) Stilton cheese, crumbled
1 tablespoon Worcestershire Sauce
2 tablespoons Guinness

4 muffins

Mix all the ingredients into a paste. Cut the muffins and toast the non cut side of the muffins. Turn the muffins over. Spread with the mixture and toast under a hot grill until it bubbles and turns golden.

Leila endured the new town for two more months before she found another job. There was a communal depression about the place which the inhabitants blamed on everything from underground gasses to electrical fields.

'I don't know what you're getting so wound up about,' Frank had said when she ranted about the drawing board dream designs so quickly cheated on by in-filling green areas, cheap materials and poor services.

'Under-floor heating, new schools, out in the country, they've never it had it so good.'

'It's sterile.'

'No one is forced to live here.'

Relief came as a small miracle via a postcard. A brown tinted picture of a Sussex priory on one side, a message on the other: '...visits are possible by written arrangement each Thursday and Tuesday afternoon. Do pop in! Sister Philomena.'

The nun's eyes shone, her radiant smile engulfed. Her walk was upright, her feet light on the gravel path looping the grounds. Although well kept there was something deliberately unlovely and gloomy about the dominance of evergreens and conifers, the absence of flowers.

'Now tell me about all your doings, how you're getting on,' the nun said as they walked the grounds. Leila wondered what the nun wanted to hear from her. She had set out on the journey to the priory without quite knowing why she as making it. She had little genuine interest in the nun.

'Do you get many visitors?' she asked for something to say.

'Too many sometimes!' the nun swooped under the low branches of a fir.

It occurred to Leila she had been invited out of some sort of charity. In her last letter from the new town to the nun she had written, 'Everyone here seems in a coma. Perhaps they put something in the water supply to keep the population from cutting their throats just for something interesting to do.'

'I'm getting on all right,' she said following on to the gravel again.

'That's the spirit,' the nun said. 'I think we'd better head back now.'

Leila had imagined the visit and return would last the day. When they were in sight of the gates again the nun unexpectedly excused herself. She was required for duties and suggested Leila explored the nearby coastal resort. 'The bus goes all the way and stops by a place that does home baking, you'll get a good lunch there, and then you can see the sea. Now you'll keep in touch. You promise me that.'

A pair of Irish girls ran the cafe the nun had recommended. One was dark haired and one was flame haired and both were tall having to stoop as they carried trays from the kitchen at street level to upper and lower floors.

A squat girl did the cooking in the back producing nostalgic high tea dishes - cinnamon fried bread, Marmite toast, creamy scrambled egg, sour milk scones with home made preserves. Leila ordered a Buck Rarebit.

'It will be a while yet,' the red-haired one took the order while collecting used crockery from an accompanying table. 'The grill has had a fit and blew itself out and we've sent out for another which is arriving any minute now. I'm using a domestic toaster but it's no joke.'

Leila looked across to the kitchen where the squat girl rushed about breaking eggs into bowls. The dark Irish girl was shouting at her. . 'Pauline I informed you ten minutes ago, there's customers dying of starvation downstairs.'

Leila rose and said she'd take a walk on the front and return later.

The sea was a pencil lead grey. Even the sea birds looked distraught with the cold. Leila folded her arms across her coat for warmth and headed into the shelter of the town centre. Cutting through side streets she passed the premises of the local evening paper. Vans were being loaded up with early editions. She walked on and passed the main entrance. An orange warmth lit the reception area behind plate glass doors. Leila returned to the doors and entered. The receptionist was collating leaflets. Leila asked if she could see the editor.

'Do you have an appointment?'

'I wondered if there were any editorial vacancies.'

'Editorial? You want the news editor,' the receptionist pressed telephone keys.

'Mr Wallace, young lady here wants to know about vacancies.'

She was directed to wait in a panelled waiting room not much larger than a sea front shelter. She picked up that day's paper. It was much like the town, breezy, easy, and unpretentious - beauty queens posed with pensioners, exclamation marks peppered the pages. A middle-aged man in flannels and horned rimmed glasses entered.

'H'm,' he said several times shuffling the paper forms. 'I gather you're here about the vacancy.'

She did not know there was a vacancy.

'I'm just enquiring.'

'What makes you want to come to us? Do you have a local connection?'

'Oh yes,' she improvised, 'One of my best friends lives in the area. She's a nun actually. Just back from Africa. She's a terrific person. Works with lepers. It's a great story.'

She could fill the forms in now or take them away and return them later. She returned to the cafe where all was now calm. The lunch crowd had left.

'It's arrived, a beautiful new grill, takes twelve full slices with no trouble,' the red haired girl announced. She remembered the order. 'A Buck Rarebit. You're in luck Pauline has only this instant made up a fresh batch of cheese mixture and the eggs are lovely.'

As Pauline set to making up the buck rarebit on the new grill. Leila began to appraise the forms. Under Job Description was typed Woman's Page Deputy Editor. By the time the Buck Rarebit arrived she had filled in the easy bits - name, age, address, education, experience.

The dark-haired Irish girl set out the cutlery while the red haired one brought over the Rarebit. The translucent poached egg sat on a plump covering of mustard yellow cheese dappled with brown and set on a square of toast. Extra triangles of buttered toast zigzagged the plate rim. She pierced the egg with a fork. The yolk of the egg was the goldenest yellow.

'It looks beautiful,' she said to the Irish girls.

'Wait till you taste it,' the red haired one smiled.

Leila cut through the toast and placed a section of egg and cheese in her mouth. The taste was an astonishing surprise.

'That made you jump didn't it?' the dark-haired girl winked.

The red-haired girl brought over jug of water. 'Not too hot for you, I hope

'It's woken me up,' Leila said.

'Pauline likes to put in three sorts of pepper. It started with a pinch but it's getting hotter by degrees. You'll have to subdue yourself Pauline,' she called over to the kitchen. 'Or we shan't have a single paying customer left!'

SISTERS' PUDDING

For 4

50 g (2 oz) short grain rice
½ litre (1 pint) full cream milk
3 camomile tea bags
2 tablespoons soft light brown sugar
Grated rind of one lemon
Handful of fresh mint
Pinch of salt
Butter
Grated nutmeg

Bring milk to the boil. Turn off the heat and add the camomile tea bags and steep for 5 - 10 minutes.
Rinse the rice and put it in a buttered ovenproof dish. Stir in the sugar, lemon rind, salt, torn mint leaves and camomile infused milk. Dot the top of the pudding with butter and grated nutmeg.
Bake uncovered in a preheated oven 300F/ 150C/ Gas mark 2 for 1 - 1½ hours, stirring once after the first 30 minutes.

When Leila arrived to take up her new post she found the woman's page office occupied by a perspiring overweight young man. His wounded-looking green eyes stared at her behind thick lenses.

'Are you the replacement?' he seemed deeply disappointed. Leila learnt that Norah Pageant, the woman's page editor was ill. The young man had been seconded from the crime desk as her replacement.

'Andrew Feathers,' he introduced himself. 'Here's your seat.' He gave the revolving chair a swift wipe.

On her arrival the news editor's secretary had been delegated to introduce Leila to the editorial staff. A few nods, indifferent handshakes, no one seemed particularly interested or curious. The woman's page was regarded by reporters as a bit of a whore, frivolous bedfellow of the supplement and advertising departments.

'What d'you reckon?' Andrew displayed the double page he was making up. The headline screamed, 'We're wired!' Two bovine-eyed blondes modelled a selection of under-wired brassieres.

Leila took over a bijou flat previously occupied by her predecessor, Vanessa Phillips, who had been snapped up by a London woman's magazine.

'She left me in a hole,' Norah Pageant had nothing good to say about Vanessa. Norah ran the page from her bed. Leila had been asked by the news editor to call in on Norah at her sea view apartment.

'She's in the dumps, take her a bunch of flowers, and put it on expenses. And promise her nothing.'

Norah, middle-aged, propped up in a green velvet chair with a rug across her legs and wearing dark glasses, was depressed.

'Well I wouldn't have chosen you,' she was frank with Leila. 'You're not at all the type for a woman's page. For a start, where's your make up?'

She gave Leila a list of contacts for instant views with a female slant on everything from childbirth to insurance. She demanded to be informed daily about what was happening to her page. 'Tell that bugger Wallace I want to see the proofs before they go out.'

Andrew Feathers dropped into Leila's office occasionally on his way back from the men's lavatories. 'Getting on all right?' he'd always ask. 'Need any help?' Sometimes he invited himself to accompany her to fashion shows and hairdressing competitions. His observations were sharp and assured.

'You're better at this than me,' Leila joked.

'Too true,' he said without a smile. Andrew, renowned for his immaculate shorthand, was the preferred choice for reporting the big court cases. He was covering the murder of a plumber by his schoolteacher girl friend. She had drowned him in the bath by holding up his legs. 'She used rubber gloves, but she still left her mark. Long fingernails, you see, pierced the rubber.'

Leila speculated whether there was a feature in murder female style.

Andrew sucked in his breath. 'Not on the woman's page. That's features. You stick to underwear and twenty ways of keeping hubby happy.'

Andrew called at her flat one evening with a bottle of gin.

'You haven't got company?' he seemed anxious and upset.

They drank the gin first with orange squash and when that ran out with Ribena. They talked and argued about politics, films and Norah's power on the woman's page. Leila's observation that Norah should keep her nose out of the page enraged Andrew.

'You know fuck all about the job,' he said, 'At least Norah cares.'

'How can you care about sleeve lengths for godssake,' the gin allowed mutual insults. Andrew asked if he could stay the night.

'I'm not interested in you,' Leila thought it best to say, 'in that way.' He wasn't interested in her. In any way. He felt too drunk, too tired to walk home. They shared her bed. He talked all night, even as Leila slept. He had hoped to be Norah's protégé. His application has been laughed at. The editor was a bastard. Norah had backed him. Wallace was a bastard. They were talking of removing Norah's name from the page. It would kill her.

'What do you want me to do about it?' Leila asked in exasperation. 'You're not trying to blame me?' she wanted to sleep.

'You make no effort. And you're cynical. You pretend.'

'No one's complained.'

'They're like you. They don't care.'

The job was a doddle. The woman's page was a kingdom of its own with access to a secretary, a photographer, an office car with a driver. Leila found herself courted by fashion buyers, hairdressers, and store owners.

'It's the best time of my life,' she wrote to the nun.

She visited her mother dressed in a light grey suit, her hair shiny and in control, her shoes delicate. A store beautician had demonstrated how to apply her make up.

'You look like a princess,' her mother said. 'Who is paying for all this?'

Leila laughed. It was all free. A mention on her page kept her groomed and dressed. She had no need to buy saucepans or linen.

They arrived at the office for her to sample. No returns necessary. She had brought a big bag of samples for her mother to use and distribute - lipsticks, hair-bands, scents, knickers, belts and brooches.

'Next time bring me a herring,' her mother said as Leila left.

Ben looked astonished. She met him at the station wearing an Italian red fitted suit and high heels. She had wanted to impress him.

He laughed: 'You look like a posh tart.'

'A tart!'

'I hardly recognised you.'

'I hardly recognised you!' She smarted from his reaction. He had lost weight and was unshaven and smelt sour

'You should,' she advised noting the shabbiness of his coat and stained shoes, 'do something about your appearance.'

'You're right,' he said.

She had taken the morning off to show him the town. Later she would take him to her flat and invite him to stay the night if he wanted. She had acquired a nifty fold up bed. There were flowers on the window ledge, three different soaps in the bathroom and a casserole dish of meat balls made from the best steak mince in a real tomato sauce ready in the oven. There were grapes in a glass dish and a bottle of robust Italian wine on a tray with matching glasses.

'Are you happy?' Ben asked as they walked the sea front.

'I've got everything I want,' she said.

'You have friends?'

'I don't have any enemies.'

There were bottle parties and booze ups. She had gone out with a reporter who turned out to be married and another who spent the evening in a drunken weep over being dropped by the editor's secretary for one of the printers.

A Canadian on overseas leave on the paper took her out to the pictures and asked her if she wanted a friendly fuck. 'No thank you,' she said.

He didn't seem to mind. 'What about some fish and chips then?'

They ate the cod and chips leaning over the promenade railings watching the waves bumping into each other.

'It's not much fun being a foreigner,' the Canadian boy said. There was grease on his moustache.

She agreed.

'You're not foreign are you?'

She didn't know what she was. Not really. It didn't seem to matter much.

Despite cleaning her teeth and soaking in a bath the taint of the fish was with her all night

'So what are you doing here?' Ben asked as they walked.

'I'm working. Building up my career. What do you think I'm doing?'

'Is it interesting?'

'It's fascinating .' She told him about the fashion shows, the recipes, and the problem page. She could do it with her eyes closed and she was being well paid. Best of all nobody was bothering her. Each day was like walking in a garden only having to decide which flowers to pick. 'I'm in heaven,' she said. Norah was still in convalescence. The rumour was she would not recover sufficiently to return to work. She had asked Leila to stop calling on her. 'I don't like your page at all. Can't stand show offs,' she had said. The sub editors had removed Norah's name from the page. 'And you can tell that bastard Wallace I'm not dead yet.'

'What are you writing about?' Ben asked.

He wouldn't be interested. The latest jewellery, neckline shape, hemline, exciting new cosmetics, lipstick colour, sixty ways to say I love you, why gossip makes a girl unpopular...

'Nothing much,' she said. 'But I get a big by line.'

'Is that important?'

'Of course it is.' It infuriated her when he pretended not to understand simple things.

'It's a reflection of how I'm regarded.'

She kept a cuttings book in her flat. She would probably not now show it to him.

'So you're writing about interesting things.'

'I'm writing rubbish,' she reverted into a childhood sulk. 'If that's what you want to hear.'

She moved ahead of him. Her confidence and pride had faded. The red suit felt common. The high heels ridiculed her attempts to walk faster. She sat on a bench facing the sea, looking down at her shoes, her jaw at a sulky angle, the sparkle gone out of her.

Ben stood opposite stretching out his hand. She turned away. He sat beside her.

'I don't want to annoy you.'

'I don't intend to stay here forever,' she said.

'I was afraid you were getting lost.'

'I'm not lost.'

'Good.'

'I'm just finding my way.'

She had been trying to be a new person and it wasn't quite working. A cultural impersonator.

They had a photograph taken together in a sea front booth and then Leila took Ben to the Irish cafe where she was now a regular customer. The dark haired girl anticipated, 'Black coffee, cinnamon toast?'

Ben wanted a glass of milk, a slice of white unbuttered bread. He had stomach ulcers.

'Is it serious?' Leila touched his hand. It was cold.

She was shaken by the sudden realisation that her brother was her anchor. And at the same time aware that if this were ever spoken he would run away from her. He was his father's son.

'You'll be all right,' she said. 'Ulcers are two a penny; I've just read an article about them. They're caused by stress, now why are you stressed...?' she droned on to cover her deep fear that without Ben she would follow her mother into a place of safe nothingness.

While Ben went to use the toilets the dark-haired girl who had been eavesdropping came over to clear the table.

'What you want for ulcers,' she advised, 'is my sister's remedy.' She wrote it down on the back of a paper bag. 'She's a nun you know and is always sitting by the dying and if there's one thing to resuscitate them it's her pudding.'

Ben had something to tell her. 'I think I've seen Pup,' he said.

He had done some relief teaching at a school. 'There was a boy there that looked like us.'

'Loads of people look like us.'

'But listen. This boy drew a picture. It was of a hut in an orange grove with a man and three children standing outside it.'

'He was a baby. He couldn't have remembered.'

'I know,' said Ben. 'It's astonishing.'

'Did you say anything to him?'

Leila knew the question was stupid as soon as she spoke it.

'His name is now James Wellington,' Ben said.

'Wellington!' Leila had not yet shed her habit of playing for time when she was troubled or confused. 'How could anyone be called Wellington!'

'He is the only child of a couple in Putney.'

'I don't suppose he knows.'

'I don't suppose he does.'

'What are we going to do?'

'Nothing.'

Leila wanted to know more. Was Pup nice? Was he happy? Was he handsome? Were his parents rich?

And: 'Are you going to see him again? Can I see him?'

'Don't be stupid,' Ben said. 'I thought you should know he's all right.'

'Well what is he like then, you can at least tell me that.'

'He's quite intelligent,' Ben said, 'But he can't draw for toffee.'

They walked the back streets uphill towards the station, past drab bookshops, stained pavements, the litter and dry sick of previous evenings outside pubs. She had to halt several times for Ben to catch his breath.

Waiting for the train with him Leila declared, 'I'm coming back to London. I'm going to find Pup.' It sounded false. It was a cover up for her panic.

'There's no point,' Ben said. 'Pup's all right. He's better off than we are.'

Watching him board the train Leila wanted to cry. He had to make two attempts to close the door. Ben had somehow lost his strength.

'Please don't let him die, please make him better and I'll do anything you ask,' she bargained with any god who might be listening.

NOT NAPOLEON'S FISH

Brazilian Cod Stew in Coconut Sauce

4 cod steaks (or other white fish)
Juice of two limes
Salt and freshly ground pepper
3 tablespoons sunflower oil
2 onions thinly sliced
1 teaspoon crushed toasted cumin
1 teaspoon crushed toasted coriander
2 green peppers, seeded and thinly sliced
2 red chillies, seeded and chopped
4 spring onions chopped
4 tablespoons chopped coriander
4 tablespoons chopped flat leaf parsley
1 800 g (14 oz) can tomatoes with juice
200 g (8 oz) creamed coconut, chopped
100 g (4 oz) coconut milk
100 g (4 oz) cooked shelled prawns

Put the fish steaks into a dish and cover with the juice of one lime and salt and pepper. Gently fry the onions until soft and pale brown and then add the cumin, dried coriander, peppers and chillies and cook for a minute, stirring. Mix in the spring onions, half the coriander and parsley, coconut cream and coconut milk. Mix thoroughly, bring to the boil and simmer for 20 mins.

Add the fish steaks and juice to the sauce. Cover and cook over a gentle heat until cooked through. Transfer the fish to a serving dish to keep warm. Bring the sauce to a boil, add the prawns, the rest of the green herbs and the lime juice and cook for 3 minutes.

Add salt and pepper to taste then pour the sauce over the fish. Serve with boiled rice.

The news editor seemed perplexed when Leila handed in her notice. She had only just received a substantial rise. He ventured the likeliest reason: 'Beckoned by the bright lights?'

'Personal reasons,' she said. She didn't think he believed her.

Ben did not seem pleased to see her. He was now staying with a married couple in a better part of London. They had two young children and another baby due soon. The wife designed fabrics in the cellar of the house and the husband taught art to maladjusted children.

'This is my sister,' Ben had introduced her. The welcome had been subdued.

'How long are you staying? As you can see, there's isn't much space.'

She was invited to share the supper. There was a heavy bean stew and brown bread. They were all vegetarians. The conversation was slow, understated. The youngest child tipped its food on to the table.

'Oh Gussie,' its mother said languidly, 'you are a mess pot' and continued a conversation about an exhibition of ceramics in Putney that was hardly worth the journey.

Leila glanced at the child who then threw a spoon at her. She picked up the spoon and scooping the mess back into the child's plate began an anecdote about once upon a time there being two hungry children who only had one piece of bread and an olive to eat all day. Her brother's kick under the table got her on the ankle. His eyes pleaded with her to drop the story and she made no further reference to the past.

'What is it you intend to do in London,' the husband asked, 'in the way of work?'

'I'm not sure,' Leila said. 'I'm a bit fed up with journalism.'

'There's modelling available at most art colleges isn't there?' the wife offered this more as an abstract notion than a question.

'I might do cooking,' Leila said. 'Or looking after children. I haven't decided.'

An extra mattress was pulled into his bedroom. 'You can sleep on the bed,' Ben insisted.

She heard him get up twice in the night. The third time it was dawn. She found him in the kitchen drinking weak tea.

'You shouldn't have come without finding somewhere to stay first,' Ben said.

'I was worried about your stomach.'

She was confident she could find a room nearby.

'Look, There's no need, I'm getting better,' he said,

Leila stayed with Ben and the artists for another week. She bought pears and bananas, grapes and oranges and arranged them on a white plate which she placed on the dresser. They were still there, untouched and unacknowledged, becoming over-ripe on the day she left.

Three applicants dressed to suggest assurance and conviction waited with cuttings books to be interviewed for the job of feature writer. The fourth was Leila who had found the advertisement only that morning and had telephoned on the off chance the vacancy was still available.

She sat waiting next to a small blonde girl with a Northern accent, her face disfigured by acne. They chatted while the men were being interviewed. The Northern girl was staying at the YWCA at the moment having only come down the day before for the interview but had two flats to look at in case she landed the job. She introduced herself as Jane Nelson, saying London was a nasty shock, everyone looked so brutal. Leila offered to accompany her on the flat hunt. She was also looking for somewhere, perhaps they could find somewhere to share.

She thought her interview had gone badly. The three interviewers asked very few questions. 'I reckon I was put in to make up the numbers,' she said to Jane as they travelled the tube to Earl's Court to view the first flat.

Jane didn't give much away about her interview. 'It's hard to tell, we'll have to wait and see,' much of her conversation was like this, platitudinous and remote, as if her interest was elsewhere.

'Are you sure you want me to come with you?' Leila finally asked as they reached their destination. 'Perhaps you prefer not to share. I don't mind. Honestly. Loads of people want to live on their own. Just say.'

'I would say. It's the last thing I want at the moment.'

The flat was on the third floor of a series of red brick mansions, unfurnished and with a double and single bedroom, a sunny sitting room, bathroom and kitchen and with immediate possession. The catch was the hefty deposit required: three months in advance.

'I couldn't find anything like that even if I got the job,' Leila said. More money would be required for furnishings and kitchen equipment.

'I've got all those,' Jane said. 'More than we'll need.'

She disclosed her story to Leila the next few weeks in pained segments.

She had been a big fish in a little pond working as a reporter in a steel manufacturing town. It was a life of parties, dances and pubs and great mates.

She had landed the most desirable bachelor in her circle, a lad who'd got away to work in the Middle East and returned a man with a worldly outlook and small fortune. Of all the girls he could have chosen he picked her. It was like something out of women's magazine fiction. They married, bought and furnished a beautiful little house and were the happiest of people. Six months later it all ended when he was accidentally shot dead by a security guard in Beirut.

The job went to Jane. A furniture van brought down her wedding gifts, her double bed, her new cooker and washing machine, her white curtains and rugs.

Leila found a job washing dishes in a nearby South American restaurant. And it was here that she first encountered Cod and Coconut. It had been the dish of the day. Two trays of it had gone quickly and were stacked for her to scour. She passed her finger across the rim where an encrustation of the dish remained and tasted it. The blend of coconut and fish stimulated memories of an air flight. When the rush was over she asked Jesus, the gentle chef, how to make the dish.

'It's my secret,' he said but the following week when he was making up another batch called her over from the sinks to observe its preparation.

It had been handed down by an uncle whose ancestor had prepared it for an Emperor. 'Napoleon?' Leila asked.

'Not Napoleon,' Jesus said. She promised to make the dish only for her own table.

Leila came home with portions of left over stews and roasted potatoes and nicked rough hands. Jane came home with half bottles of Scotch and shouting men who messed up the toilet and stayed late. Leila did not feel she could complain. It was not her flat.

One night when she was asleep one of Jane's friends strayed into Leila's room and climbed into bed with her. Leila felt outraged by his pawing and the smell of beer and vomit on him. She kicked and pushed but there was no moving him out of her bed. Within a few minutes he was lying belly down asleep and snoring. Leila pulled a blanket from under his legs and left the room. She approached Jane's door intending to shout at her. The noise from Jane's room was too intimate to interrupt without embarrassment. Leila trudged into the sitting room. The sofa was already occupied by a young man reading a book. He looked up.

'D'you live here?' he asked. His name was Edmund. He had a strange accent.

'You're Australian,' she guessed. Earl's Court was jumping with Australians doing Europe. He was English, a journalist on leave from East Africa. He had been brought to the flat by a couple of South African colleagues, friends of Jane's.

'Are you a journalist as well?' he asked.

'I'm a cook,' she said, 'at the moment.'

On their first, second and fourth date he took her out to a pub. On the third date it was a wine bar. He was not interested in food but under pressure agreed to go out for a meal. Leila insisted it would be her treat. She wanted him to try a very special dish made by a friend from an ancient recipe.

There was a jazz club below the restaurant. 'We could go there afterwards,' she suggested. He was not keen. But if she really wanted to. She knew before the meal arrived that it was a mistake.

The cod and coconut dish was perfection. The chef had evolved a way of serving a pyramid of fragrant rice to accompany the dish. The cod snuggled alongside tomato wedges energised with green chillies. Edmund glanced at the dish with deep suspicion.

He tasted it cautiously. Leila watched him gamely swallow one morsel with another and then place his knife and fork together. 'Let's order some more wine,' he said.

'You don't like it?'

It was not his kind of thing.

'It's only fish.'

'I know,' he said, 'I'm sorry. I just can't eat it His tone said 'subject closed'. Leila could not leave it.

'What do you enjoy eating?' Steak, a mixed grill, roasts, chicken, things he could recognise, that hadn't been mucked about with.

'What about fish?'

'Fried fish is all right,' he conceded, 'from a fish and chip shop. Can we talk about something else?'

'You're impossible,' she said.

'No, I'm an Englishman. English people like English food. What's wrong with that?'

'But you live in Africa.'

'Some of the best roast dinners I've had have been in Africa.'

'I wouldn't go all the way to Africa for a roast dinner,' she said.

They looked at each other like a zebra might glance at a giraffe - curious, unthreatening, able to occupy the same space in slightly puzzled amiability.

UTAH'S FRIED CAULIFLOWER

A cauliflower
A knob of butter
A little vegetable oil
An onion cut into thin rings
1 egg, beaten and seasoned with salt and pepper
Celery seeds

Lightly boil the cauliflower in salted water, drain well. Break into sprigs. Heat the butter and oil in a frying pan.

Add the onion and celery seeds and fry for a few minutes until soft but not too brown. Now dip the cauliflower florets in the beaten egg and add to the pan, turn with a spatula.

Plate up and serve.

When Leila told Ben she was moving to Africa to marry he asked her if she was pregnant. He knew where she could obtain an abortion. There was no need to run away

'I wouldn't go to Africa to have a baby!' she protested stung by his assumption.

'Who is this character you intend to marry?' Ben asked. They were in his studio. Eyeless life size masks of Greek statues hung from walls.

'He's an Englishman,' she said.

'Why Africa?'

'He works there.'

'How long have you known him?'

It had been less than a month. He had taken her out to a couple of cinemas and a Becket play and then suggested sailing on the Norfolk Broads.

'Where's that?' she asked.

'In Norfolk! Don't tell me you can't sail.'

'I can't even swim.'

He looked at her as if she were a Martian.

'Doesn't matter,' he said, 'if you fall in I'll jump in and save you.' This was what she thought she liked about him, his lack of interest in doom. It may have been a failure of imagination. He did not anticipate or invite problems. He expected things to work out.

'My father's in prison,' she said on their first day on the boat. 'And my mother's in a mad house. Would you like to meet them?'

'Not particularly.' The weather had turned grim. They were both miserable with the cold. He had forgotten how cruel March could be and she had never given it a thought. Everything in the boat was damp. Within two days Edmund was sneezing and shivering.

They heard from a publican that three miles away a honeymoon couple had drowned. 'She fell in and the silly bugger jumped in after her with his wellingtons on.'

'Shall we go back?' Leila suggested.

'Why?'

'It's obvious. You're ill.'

'I'll be all right. What about you?'

'Nothing wrong with me,' she replied.

They both returned with high temperatures.

Jane said it was a hoot.

'Anyone would think you'd been to the North Pole.'

The flat was a good place to recuperate during the day when Jane was at work. At night it became an after pub tipping out time extension venue which did not quieten until the early hours. One morning Leila found Jane lying in a bath of cold water her skin creped from the long soaking. She shook her and pulled her by the hair screaming, 'Open your eyes!'

Jane blinked and with her foot pulled out the plug and yawned.

'Do stop shouting, I've got a massive headache.'

'I thought you were dead,' Leila said.

'I fell asleep, that's all. You do dramatise.'

A month after their return from Norfolk Leila received a postcard from Edmund with a stamp of a grazing zebra. He was in the tropics. 'When are you coming out,' it asked with two neat question marks.

Jane lent Leila the money for the airfare. They had calculated it would take four months to save for it, three if she worked overtime and the tips were good. Now that she was leaving they had become closer friends.

There had been complaints about the nightly rackets and the empty bottles left out in the hall. 'You're getting yourself a bad reputation,' Leila said. It was a Sunday morning. Jane having planned to travel home to visit her parents had woken too late to make the journey viable. 'We'll get chucked out.'

'I don't care,' Jane said. 'I don't care a damn about any of that. Drink, fuck and be happy, that's my motto, what's yours?'

'To keep going I suppose.'

'What for?' Jane was making up a gin and tonic. It was barely midday. 'What for?' her voice was scathing.

Leila didn't know. She said: 'So as not to go under.' She corrected this: 'In the hope of arriving... somewhere.'

Jane laughed: 'Who are you kidding!'

After two more gins Jane confessed she had moved to London to die. Leila said she didn't believe her. But in her heart she knew it was true.

Ben asked Leila to meet him. He had now moved in with a model from the art school called Utah. 'She just lets me sleep here when her husband is away, so don't get any funny ideas,' he said. Utah's husband was a merchant sailor. 'She drinks, so she's always broke.' There were canvases of Utah's seal-like body propped up against the walls in the sitting room. The house smelt of stale brassicas.

He had prepared a dish of fried cauliflower which Utah had taught him. They sat opposite each other at the kitchen table. Ben sawed slices from a brown loaf sprinkled with cumin seeds.

'The thing is,' Ben said and stopped to cough. Leila noticed his bitten down nails.

He hardly touched his food.

'Is it your ulcers again?' she asked. He looked grey.

'No. I'm tired that's all. I can't sleep.'

'Is it your work?'

'It's him.'

'Dad?'

'He wants us to be together again. To live in the house. And I can't do it.'

Leila said: 'Neither can I.'

Ben snorted.

'I would if I wasn't going to Africa.'

'Look, Dad is getting out and one of us has to take him in.'

'Why?'

'You know why. He can't be alone.'

'You're his favourite.' Leila regretted the reproach as soon as it was uttered. His favourite and now his tormentor. She could hear the bitter endless wail which would follow Ben even into his dreams. 'What I done for you, what I sacrificed, for you, for you, not your mother, your sister, your small brother, you, the boy, my eldest son and now you turn your back, now you are ashamed, ashamed of your father, you don't want to recognise me, may you rot in hell, may you be cursed a thousand times and a thousand times again, for the knife you have put in my heart....'

'I can't stand him.'

'Couldn't mum -'

'Not yet.'

'She's better. She's well enough. Has anybody asked her?'

'I asked her. She won't until there's a house.' He cruelly mimicked Mrs Adon's Teutonic tones. 'I want a table and four chairs; I want a gas cooker with four rings. I want lino on the floor. I want sheets on the bed. You get me those, I go to Timbuktu.'

Ben bit his nails. 'He wants you to visit him.'

He handed her a slip of paper. It was a visiting order for the end of the month.

Leila said: 'I won't be here.'

'In Africa!' Mrs Adon laughed. 'Can't you run away any further?'

Leila had brought her a leather handbag as a goodbye present. Inside was a comb, a mirror and a batch of photographs in a docket. Leila set out the photographs like a pack of cards. Mrs Adon's interest was in the mirror one side of which was magnified. With it she examined her teeth, her chin and the rim of one eyelid.

'Who is this?' Leila held up a photograph of Ben.

'It's Ben, isn't it?'

Her mother considered but did not commit an opinion.

'And this is me, and this is me and Ben and Dad and you're wearing your summer suit. And this is Edmund. Edmund lives in Africa.'

Mrs Adon wasn't interested.

'Where is Pup?' she asked, 'I don't see Pup.'

PAW PAW

Paw Paw (Papaya) with lime

Delicious for breakfast

The ripe paw paw is yellow orange and soft when ripe. Cut it in half, the fruit has a deep apricot coloured flesh which is sweet and aromatic. Scoop out the black seeds and sprinkle with lime juice.

The Jacarandas were past their best when Leila arrived in Africa. Their dusky blue droppings coloured the pavements. Edmund's flat was in the city centre. He drove her there in a battered Citroen straight from the airport. The light was so bright it hurt her eyes.

'You'll want to sleep,' he said. The flat was plain and cool. He drew the curtains. He'd be back from the paper in a couple of hours.

After he left she walked through the flat on bare feet. A typical bachelor's flat, sparse, clean enough, unloved. It smelt of something sweet and slightly rotting. She traced it to a wooden bowl of fruit. She immediately recognised the pineapple. The other fruits were strange. There was an overhead shower rose in the bathroom and minimal toiletries, a wooden duckboard. She showered under cold water and then realised there was no towel. She wrapped herself in a dressing gown from her suitcase and lay on the top of Edmund's bed in the darkened room. She could hear the sound of traffic and voices. She turned on the radio to hear tribal dancing music. She slept for a long time dreaming of her little brother waddling in bare feet on the concrete floor of the hut in the orange grove. She was woken by a persistent tapping noise.

'I'm awake,' she mumbled. Assuming it was Edmund and irritated that he'd woken her, she turned over with a sigh and closed her eyes. She still felt sleepy and heavy-eyed. She heard the sound of a cup shaking in a saucer and opened her eyes to see a pair of bare brown feet at her bedside.

'Tea, memsahb.' A slightly built African with greying hair was setting down a green cup and saucer on the bedside table. A moment later she heard him padding out and gently closing the door.

Leila sat in bed sipping the tea. She could hear the African moving about. She set her suitcase on the bed and began to unpack. She heard Edmund's voice talking Swahili. She found him in the kitchen talking and laughing with the African.

'What are you saying?'

'He wants to know whether you are my wife or my mistress.'

'What did you say?'

'Told him to mind his own business. Are you up to going out?'

'Now?' She needed to unpack, iron a dress.

'Chingili will do that,' Edmund said. He looked browner and taller than she remembered.

'I don't know what I'm doing here,' she said.

'Yes, you do.'

If she had, she had not yet shaped it into words.

'I feel as if I'm dreaming.'

He took her to the Sans Chique, a crowded dilapidated restaurant bar owned by noisy Italians and patronised by Edmund's male colleagues. White men in shorts and long beige socks, Africans in suits. Asian men in blazers with badges. The few women who were there were assured, glamorously attired.

'Edmund's bride,' the word went round.

They drank Tusker beer and dined on enormous steaks crowded with chips and vegetables.

'I can't eat all this,' Leila complained. There was meat on her plate to feast a family of four in England.

'It's too much.'

'Meat costs nothing here.'

It was the same at breakfast. She could smell the frying as she dressed. Bacon, eggs, sausage, fried bread.

'I can't eat a cooked breakfast,' she said as Edmund came out of the shower.

'You feeling all right?'

'Fine. I just don't like it.' It sounded rejecting.

She heard him shout to Chingili in Swahili.

'It's nothing personal.'

'I didn't think it was.'

'Does he do all the cooking?'

'He'll do whatever you tell him. Within reason. Take him to the market with you and he'll carry your stuff.'

'Does he speak English?'

'He understands as much as he wants to. He's been with me three years. You'll be all right.'

'I could do the cooking and cleaning,' she said. It would be a way of contributing until she found paid work.

'Chingili has four children up-country to keep,' Edmund said. 'He doesn't cost much.'

They sat at the dining table end to end waiting. It had been set with napkins folded into lilies and with nasturtiums floating in a glass bowl.

'No wonder he's late, Chingili! sasa hivi,' Edmund shouted.

Chingili entered slowly in his stiff off-white uniform and plimsolls carrying a tray.

He brought over a cooked breakfast for Edmund and a plate of paw paw with wedges of lime for Leila. The paw paw was an unknown fruit for her. It looked like pumpkin and tasted faintly of melon. The texture was dry. 'Scented cardboard,' Leila thought. The lime juice gave it some bite.

'It looks unripe,' Edmund said. 'You'll find some good ones in the market.'

'You will go shopping with Memsahb this morning,' Edmund instructed the houseboy. He handed Leila money. 'You're expected to haggle.'

She walked with him to the front door and whispered. 'Does he have to come with me?'

'Look,' he said, 'he's as nervous of you as you are of him. Give him a break.'

Leila and Chingili walked in uneasy silence through the noisy streets. She had tried a few conversational openings. 'Is the market far away?' and 'It's getting hotter.' The morning cool was giving way to a glaring brightness. Chingili's response was a muted 'Yes Memsahb.' They walked through a street of dusty shops selling spices and then through the meat market. Carcasses of goat, sheep and cow were being hacked and sawed, chopped and minced by men in bloodied aprons shouting 'Lovely, lovely, lovely, all good and fresh today. Come, Madame see.' Blobs of black flies hovered and sat over the joints and were flicked away by small boys equipped with cowtail fly whisks.

The Fish market was smaller, wet, a smell of ammonia and decomposition. The plaintive eyes of small and large warm water and lake fish stared from marble counters.

'Which is good?' Leila asked Chingili.

He shrugged, seeming embarrassed to be seen with her. She raised her voice:

'Which does Edmund like?'

Chingili pointed. 'This one.' he almost whispered it. It was called Kingfish.

'Enough for two,' Leila said in slow English to the smiling African never taking his eyes off her as he brought down his knife through the fish.

'What else do we need?' she wanted to get out of there.

'We need sugar, we need soap.'

'You get it,' she heard herself telling it to Edmund: she had not come to Africa to shop.

Chingili looked depressed.

'I cannot.' A slight figure in white shorts, his eyes down. His glumness and the smell of rotting fruit reminded her of something. The orange grove. Her father searching his pockets for coins. The meal with a handful of olives.

'Why? Why can't you?'

He seemed unable to say. And then she knew. He hadn't got the money.

She opened her purse. 'Take what you need,' she said. He looked blank. She tipped coins on to her palm and then added a note.

He pointed to the ones he wanted and waited for her to place them in the palm of his hand. This way there would be no possibility of accidental or unintentional touch.

AHMED'S SKEWERS

Kofta Kebabs

Serves 6

1 kg (2 lbs) lamb
2 grated onions
Large bunch chopped fresh parsley
Large bunch chopped fresh mint
1 teaspoon cinnamon
1 teaspoon paprika
Salt and freshly ground pepper

Blend all the ingredients into a paste. With wet hands, take portions of meat and wrap them around a flat bladed skewer. Press into a flat sausage shape. Grill for 5 - 8 minutes, turning once.

Edmund left early each day and returned during the houseboy's afternoon break for a sandwich, to sleep with Leila, to shower and change his clothes before returning to work.

Leila usually lay in bed until she heard the houseboy letting himself in to bring in the washing and start the ironing.

'Can't he do it downstairs?' she had asked, wanting the flat to herself.

From the back window there was a view of the houseboys' quarters. Wood smoke and laughter wafted up. She had seen these 'boys' below pegging and folding laundry, beating sisal mats.

'He could, if you provide him with a charcoal iron.' There was no electricity in the quarters. The cooking was done on a charcoal stove.

'No electricity? That's ridiculous.'

'It's how it is.'

Leila couldn't get used to living with a servant. She was always aware of Chingili in the flat. 'Excuse me memsahb,' he'd say entering the room with wax polish and sheepskin pads. At first she watched him skate over the wooden floor on the sheepskin pads - with minimal movement, as silently as possible. Her attempts at conversation with him were awkward and she felt unwelcome. He looked trapped when she invited him to say whether he preferred wax or liquid polish. It was clear what he wanted was to get on with the work and then get out into the safety of his quarters. After a while she vacated the room when he entered.

She'd sit on the bed with a book waiting for the sound of the floor mats being beaten on the veranda wall and then for the tap on the door. 'Excuse me memsahb,' entering the room with dusters and a broom.

She took to walking back to the office with Edmund. For the exercise, she claimed. To explore the shops. Buy postcards. She killed time in hotel coffee bars and sometimes caught a certain look from the silent African waiters and felt vulnerable.

She needed a job. For a job she needed a work permit.

'When are we getting married?' she risked the question one afternoon.

'When I get a day off.'

Most of the newspaper wives were accommodated out of town in the bigger company flats. She was invited to tea. She had yet to learn to drive. 'Take a taxi,' Edmund suggested, 'I'll pick you up from there.'

It was early December. A time for warm coats and boots in England. In Africa the white women kept cool in floral dresses, dark glasses and sandals.

Bridget and two women friends were in the sitting room blanching almonds for marzipan and drinking home-made lemonade. A housegirl was cleaning the oven.

'Wouldn't be Christmas without marzipan,' Bridget was saying. She was wearing a home-made apron over a Liberty lawn home-made dress. 'Do you sew?' she asked Leila. The sprigged upholstered covers, the lined curtains, the velvet crimped cushions, the tasselled lampshades, the tapestry picture of a pair of setters was all Bridget's handiwork.

'I can cook,' Leila said, 'a bit.'

'You must get a sewing machine. Save yourself pounds,' Bridget said. 'The local stuff is cheap and nasty and the imported clothes are far too expensive for what they are. It's not difficult, I'll help you.'

She had not come to Africa, Leila told herself, to wear Simplicity Pattern dresses.

The women she met at Press receptions were generally grander but less welcoming - the wives of and daughters of plantation owners, embassy employees, doctors and university lecturers. At the clubs she met wayward hospital nurses and the wives and girl friends of crop spraying pilots and railway engineers.

There was an unexpected invitation to the home of a sub editor on the paper. A local resident, Al Ahmed, had just been promoted to chief sub over the heads of imported white men.

'Do you want to go?' Edmund asked. 'I don't know that there will be many people we know there.'

Ahmed's house was in the Asian area. It was a pink ice cream colour on two floors with ragged bougainvillaea in unpainted oil drums fronting the grille-gated entrance. Leila was the only European woman there. She was offered a sherbet flavoured drink and chatted with the men until she realised that other than an aged granny on a chair, the other women were gathered at one end of the room. They were dressed in subtle silks, their hair was oiled and they covered their mouths when they laughed.

She joined them and was offered food from a metal tray lined with a banana leaf. She chose a skewer of spiced and fragrant meat. It reminded her of another time.

'I wish I could make this,' she said. The women took her to the kitchen and delighted in giving her an animated demonstration.

Leila spent a morning tracking down a list of spices and lamb from an Arab butcher. She had sent Chingili to find a banana leaf.

She watched Edmund ease the kebabs from a skewer on to his plate. He swallowed a mouthful and called to Chingili in the kitchen.

He swallowed another mouthful.

'You don't like it?'

'It's all right.'

'Just all right! If you don't like it, don't force yourself,' she got up and moved his plate away.

'I didn't say I didn't like it.'

'It's taken me all morning to make.' How had she landed up with someone who was not interested in food!

'I'd prefer something different, that's all.'

'Like what?'

'Like a pork chop,' he said as Chingili brought in the cheese and biscuits.

Leila sent a post card of a banana tree to Ben and wrote: 'Africa is quite exotic.'

A CAKE OF FRUIT

Tropical Fruit Platter

This dish is extraordinarily impressive at the end of a meal. It involves no cooking, just assembling pieces of fruit. The idea is that you can sample all the different pieces of fruit and use your fingers for everything without getting them wet or sticky

Find an interestingly – shaped large plate or platter. Cover with large fresh leaves e.g. vine, sycamore, so that the leaves droop over the edges. Cut up fruit and arrange in little mounds and cascades. The following selection of fruit works well. For it to look attractive vary the height and keep disparate little piles, don't mix them up.

1 pineapple cut in half width wise. Cut the bottom half into rounds and then quarters, then lay in three or four rows. Leave the top half uncut and stand it up as the centrepiece of the platter
4 oranges cut into 6, keeping skin on
4 Kiwi fruit, skin and cut into thick slices
1 melon, cut into slices with skin on
6 passion fruit, cut in half
2 starfruit sliced and arranged in little stacks
Pack of physalis distributed in little mounds
Lychees distributed in little heaps with skins on
Fresh dates distributed in small clusters
Red or black grapes into tiny bunchlets

They were to be married tomorrow. Tomorrow! The Registrar's office had an unexpected slot available.

They had moved from the flat to an out of town colonial bungalow with suspended floors and a tin roof. The grounds were modest with tall gates and small servants' quarters within shouting distance. As she could not drive the bungalow was less convenient than the flat but it meant Leila could enjoy her own garden. Two flame trees were its main attraction. Its previous owner, an elderly schoolteacher, had returned to England to nurse her ailing mother. The hardy Kikuyu grass lawn and octagonal flowerbeds were a testament to her sense of order. They required little maintenance.

Chingili introduced a 'sister' as a suitable garden girl. By now Leila knew the necessity for employing a garden girl was not the issue. There was an unstated obligation, the girl needed the job. Her name was Wambui.

'Is she your wife?' Leila asked Chingili when she saw Wambui enter his quarters.

'She is not my wife.'

'She's not your sister though.' Chingili did not reply.

'Is she your girl friend?'

'She is a cousin.'

'She is no more your cousin than I am!'

Why did it matter?

'I don't like being lied to,' Leila tried to justify her anger.

'Then don't ask questions he doesn't want to answer.' Edmund's attitude towards Chingili was friendly indifference. He'd issue commands, 'Iron my shirt, bring a beer, close the windows' and Chingili would usually obey. At the end of each month he was paid.

If he needed a loan or a day off, it was negotiated. They left each other alone to work through their particular roles seemingly without acrimony or tension.

'He doesn't want a relationship. Try and ignore him.' It was difficult at first.

Leila was befriended by the wife of an advertising brand manager who lived in a beautiful colonial-style house with a swimming pool, stables and guesthouse. She employed four house servants including an ayah to care for her two children. Leila watched the ayah pushing a white child to and fro on a creaking swing. The ayah was a Luo, lake people known for a certain moroseness.

'Your ayah doesn't look very happy,' Leila observed.

'Doesn't she? I haven't looked at her today,' the child's mother said and asked Leila if she preferred milk or lemon with her tea.

On the morning of the wedding Edmund left for work in a rush promising to send Len Shersby, a rotund colleague, to take her shopping. Len and Jim Rodriguez, a photographer on the newspaper, had been roped in the night before as best men and witnesses. Shopping for what? For the wedding party. He had no idea how many were coming. He had yet to invite them. 'What about my hair?'

'Your hair's fine.' He ruffled it and laughed. 'It will be all right,' he promised.

'Won't I need a ring!' she called after Edmund as drove towards the gate.

He had forgotten. He'd meet her in the Sans Chique. One o'clock.

'This is mad,' she said.

Len, a middle-aged Yorkshireman, arrived an hour late. His car had been involved in a prang with a drinks lorry. He had a military attitude, giving orders and expecting instant obedience. 'Hop into the motor chop chop.'

He then threw a series of orders to Chingili in Swahili. 'Told him to get his finger out, tart the place up for his master's wedding.'

First stop supermarket. Len had automatically taken charge of the catering. Leila felt there was little time or point in countermanding him. They were running late. 'Throw in anything you like the look of,' he instructed, lobbing tins of sardines, pate, ham, sausages, bagfuls of bread rolls, tomatoes, a fistful of cucumbers, several lettuces, a side of salmon and a rope of sausages links.

'Find another trolley,' he barked. 'We need booze.'

A gaggle of African boys helped carry the booty into Len's car. He would drive the groceries to the house while Leila took a taxi to meet Edmund. Leila then remembered the cake: they did not have a wedding cake. It was too late to return to the shops.

'Your houseboy can knock up a cake, surely.' She was not sure.

'What kind of cake?' She supposed a fruitcake.

She was three quarters of an hour late for the rendezvous. Edmund was in a bad mood. 'Where the hell have you been?'

'Shopping!' she snapped at him.

The shops were about to close for lunch and they had not yet selected a ring. 'Quick,' he shouted. The first jewellery shop had already closed. He ran ahead to another. Leila lagged behind, hot and annoyed.

'Come on!' he called. He had found a shop. The Asian owner was locking up, and was persuaded to remain open for another ten minutes. The rings were all fine but none fitted. Leila's fingers had swollen from the heat and excitement of the morning. 'We can stretch,' the shop owner promised. 'You come back in fifteen minutes, it will fit.'

They waited in the Sans Chique with a beer.

'Come to my party,' Edmund invited friends and acquaintances in the bar. 'I'm getting married. Today.'

It was clear Edmund had little idea how many people were expected at the wedding. Maybe fifty, maybe a hundred. Married Europeans needed to confirm with wives, Asians were vague about family commitments, Africans tended to extend invitations to tenuous relatives and acquaintances.

The ring still did not quite fit. It would have to do. 'The lady must put her hands in icy water,' the jeweller's doe-eyed daughter advised from the back of the shop. She had a gift for the bridal couple, a sprig of fragrant frangipani wrapped in green tissue paper. 'Happiness for your day,' she said.

They arrived at the bungalow to find it deserted. Shopping bags covered the kitchen floor. They were due at the Registrar's office within half an hour. Leila called out for Chingili. There was no response. She ran to the servants' quarters. 'Chingili, Wambui!' The doors of the quarters were locked. A young African girl, a 'sister' of

Wambui who sometimes stayed in the quarters was in the shower house washing her feet.

'Where are they?' Leila shouted at her. 'Chingili and Wambui. I need them in the house.' The African girl replied in Swahili, pointing to the road.

Edmund was showering when Leila returned. She walked into the kitchen with some notion of beginning to prepare the food for the party and realised it was impossible. There was no time.

She switched on the radio: Jamhuri tribal music. She closed her eyes.

'Turn off that racket,' Edmund had changed into a suit and was knotting a tie. He'd left the shower running for her. 'I'm going mad,' she said. 'Chingili has disappeared, there's food going bad, I've got a splitting headache...'. Edmund pushed her into the bathroom. 'Calm down' he said. 'It will be fine.' At that moment heavy drops of summer rain began drumming on the tin roof of the bungalow. As they approached the car Leila saw Chingili enter the back door. Edmund started the engine. Leila said 'Two minutes!' and ran back to the bungalow one hand over her hair.

'Chingili,' she demonstrated like a manic comic, 'this, the pate, the smoked salmon the Motadello...this to go on this, the bread, rolls, biscuits...do you understand?' In the car Edmund said 'Leila'.

'What?'

'You look beautiful.'

She smiled: 'So do you.'

They arrived at the Registrar's Office damp, laughing and panting like children who had raced past a water hose. Len, in an ancient suit, and Jim, equipped with camera and flash were already there.

'You've cut it fine matey,' Len, a drinking pal of the Registrar, had begged time for them. The office should have closed at one o'clock. It was now just after half past.

Leila sent her mother and brother each a photograph of the ceremony, ostensibly capturing the familiar tender moment in which the bridegroom slips the ring on to the bride's finger.

The Registrar had watched with raised eyebrows as Edmund attempted and failed to accomplish this task. Leila winced as he turned and pushed the ring on. It did not fit.

'I dare say it can be stretched,' the Registrar said glancing at his watch. It was way past time for his afternoon nap.

The wedding party returned to the bungalow to find it crammed with garden flowers. Containers of all description had been commandeered - toothbrush mugs, a measuring jug, saucepans, beer bottles and a bucket. The flowers, Leila discovered later from frozen looks and terse notes had been 'borrowed' by Chingili and his cousin from neighbourhood gardens.

Guests began to arrive in threes and fours. In the kitchen Chingili and his cousin were still at work preparing food. They had used their imagination to overcome the insufficiency of crockery and silverware. Banana leaves lined planks of wood, frying pans and container lids. Leila smiled. 'Very good,' she said to Chingili. 'Very artistic.'

Her face dropped as she examined the items of food more closely. A beautifully towered pastry round contained layers of incompatible ingredients - ham topped with mashed sardines speared with a mini frankfurter. Halved boiled eggs smeared with guava jam and sprinkled with pea nuts.

She moved into the sitting room to find Edmund. The suspended wooden floor was a-bounce with an assortment of Africans, their wives, brothers, colleagues, messenger boys, drinking beer from bottles and tucking into the snacks Chingili's cousin offered from what Leila recognised as the bathroom duckboard lined with leaves. A sprinkling of Europeans and Asians wives including Bridget, resplendent in a Vogue pattern two-piece with a huge taffeta bow on her bosom, occupied the settee and looked on knowingly while their men downed beers. Edmund was at the door greeting another carload of Africans.

'Where is the bride?' Leila was asked by a series of strangers.

'Where's the cake?'

Edmund echoed the question to Leila who shrugged. He shouted to Chingili passing round more of his improbable stacked snacks: 'Where's our wedding cake? '

Chingili returned from the kitchen with the fruit cake he had made. It was a wonderful assemblage of slices of every available fruit. Circles of pineapple were topped with guavas and paw paw, skirted by bananas, strawberries, custard apple balls, bejewelled with black and white grapes and skinned orange and grapefruit slices. The whole was topped by a tomato. There was applause and then drum music began to pound.

HINDI TEA

Spicy Tea

This fragrant tea can be drunk after a meal. It is both very warming as a winter drink and cooling in hot climates.

300 ml (½ pint) milk
½ pint water
2 teabags
2 cinnamon sticks
2 cardamom pods
1 clove
Sugar if liked

Bring the milk and water to boil in a saucepan, and then add the teabags and spices. Boil for a further 3-5 minutes. Strain into a teapot. Serve with or without sugar.

Now that she was married Leila did not require a work permit. She found a morning job freelancing as a copywriter with an advertising agency. Her first project was Parker Pens, the double arrowed status symbol favoured by the armies of messenger boys servicing the city offices. A simple survey revealed that there were more Parker pens clipped into the shirt pockets of clerical workers than were ever produced in the factory in England.

   A messenger in the agency spilled the beans. You could buy a Parker Pen top for a few cents in the bazaar. Leila devised a series of advertisements in which locals brought in to take over the vacancies left by departing Europeans were depicted writing with a fountain pen.

'You've been Africanised' became a familiar farewell to expatriates.

Edmund's job produced the usual perks - invitations to embassies and High Commission receptions, free meals in new restaurants. In the early days of post independence the development and tourist industries were set to boom. Everyone wanted editorial mentions, there was a feeling of apprehensive excitement about which way the country would go. Bridget set up an exclusive service to groom village girls who suddenly found themselves occupying ministerial premises into the rights and wrongs of table settings, lavatory chain mechanics, appropriate dress and presentation for greeting overseas VIPs.

Leila was to write an article for the prestige house magazine of a multi-national company to illustrate the contribution made to national independence and development. Johnson Ndugu, a newly recruited African executive, would accompany her on the tour of the territory. A diesel Mercedes would be provided for the five day safari.

'You lucky devil ,' Edmund looked over the itinerary. 'You'll see the Mountains of the Moon, Lake Magadi, the Turkana...the real Africa.'

Johnson was a muted and considerate driver, a nervous companion. Barring one occasion when he lost total control, he remained subdued throughout their journey. Leila imagined he had been briefed not to touch, become familiar with or in any way offend. Despite splashings of aftershave Johnson had about him the acrid strong sweat smell of African men. She had complained to Edmund of Chingili's smell about the house.

'Apparently we smell pretty awful to them,' he pointed out. 'You'll get used to it.' She never did.

They drove in awkwardness through the spectacular vast territory of forests, rocks and sand, heat and sudden downpours of rain. Johnson's formal responses to her questions concerning company marketing strategies and policies were articulate and clear.

The questions Leila threw at him regarding his family circumstances, his job, his hopes, seemed to make him uncomfortable. He either did not reply at all or pointed out a feature in the far distance.

'Bomas, we will visit them today.'

The soil here was a uniform murram red. On the road they passed women carrying water, children herding cattle, giraffe and zebra herds.

'You cannot eat zebra,' Johnson Ndugu replied in answer to her question on the subject, 'unless you are a lion.'

'What do you like to eat?' she asked to make conversation. He seemed not to understand her meaning. 'Meat or fish or what?'

'I eat many foods,' he said. 'When I am hungry.'

The boma was an extraordinary circle of conical roofed huts huddled on a vast plain. Johnson was greeted with shouts and cries as he and Leila climbed out of the Mercedes.

'Here you will see that I am taking future orders for our products,' Johnson announced. Parker pen and order book in hand and with his blazer buttoned he stepped confidently toward a dusty mud hut outside which an old man in a loin cloth worked an ancient treadle sewing machine. Naked children, their faces studded with flies, bare breasted women wearing wire jewellery gazed and kept their distance as Leila approached in her London frock and sandals.

The stock in the shop comprised small packets of sugar in blue paper, five bars of soap, aspirin sold in single tablets, matches and oil from a tin drum.

Johnson conversed in the dark hut with the shop owner, an elderly man in a wrap sporting a flywhisk. 'What is he saying?' Leila asked intermittently. Johnson's translations were vague. 'We are discussing business matters.'

When they drove away she asked for details of the transaction.

'This time he has ordered nothing. He has no money. Maybe next time he will take some soap.'

A day's drive later they visited an up country township where some fifty women patiently awaited a demonstration of Sunlight soap. Several of the children had been named Omo, Sunlight and Persil.

The demonstration team, three uniformed women got up to look like nurses and equipped with bright yellow plastic bowls and buckets of water, began the proceedings by leading the communal singing of the Sunlight soap commercial. Bars of soap were stacked on a cloth-covered table.

These free samples were what the women had walked miles for. To obtain them they went through the ritual of singing and dancing, applauding the demonstrations of how to correctly wash parts of the body and lectures on basic hygiene. The reward often extended to leaflets and cardboard point- of- sale material which came in handy as dung and flour scoops, sun hats, back scratchers, for fire making and domestic decoration.

The agency had booked Leila and Johnson into a failing tourist lodge. It was out of season and in mid renovation. Its main feature was a treetop bar on decking circling a huge baobab tree. It looked out onto an artificial water hole attracting wild life for the tourists to film.

'I am expecting someone,' she said to a hovering waiter in the dining room. She waited in the bar for a while and then sent a messenger to make enquiries. The waiter returned to say Mr Ndugu was not in his room.

Leila waited another quarter of an hour and then began her meal alone.

After dinner she asked the receptionist if Mr Ndugu had returned.

The receptionist did not know. Leila joined an elderly English couple at the treetop bar. They were returning to England after forty years of coffee growing.

'It's all over bar the shouting,' the man said. 'They don't want us here any more.'

She told them about the article she was writing.

They seemed completely uninterested.

At the far end of the bar steps led to lower platform providing a view of the distant mountains. Beneath it were the hotel staff quarters. The smell of charred meat and smoke wafted up. Looking through the slats Leila saw Johnson on the steps with a plate of food. The receptionist and waiter were sitting on stools drinking beer from a bottle.

In the morning Johnson explained his absence at dinner by saying he had business commitments.

Closer to the Lake they visited two Asian brothers running a roadside store selling everything from bicycle tyres to Java cloth and zinc buckets. Johnson spoke to them in English introducing Leila; 'a famous writer for our company'. Leila was feeling slightly sick. The roads had been winding and the sky overcast. 'Soon there will be the long rains,' Johnson predicted. 'We must finish before they start because the road will be bad.'

The youngest Asian man had nice teeth and a cockney accent.

'Fancy a cup of tea?' he asked. He dusted down a chair and barked in Swahili to an African to make tea. His name was Prem. He'd begun a course at the London School of Economics, cut short when his father and brother were butchered with pangas on the airport road.

While the elder brother took Johnson to a shed behind the shop to look over a Land Rover he was willing to sell at a good price, Prem asked Leila about London. He had lived in Ealing. 'I never once saw a sunset. The traffic gave me asthma .'

As they waited for the tea he played Leila his favourite record, a scratchy version of 'Yesterday' by the Beatles.

'So what are you doing by yourself out here?' he asked 'In the middle of nowhere.'

'Working,' she said, 'taking a look at different things.'

There was a sound of shouting.

'They're waiting for us,' she thought he meant Johnson Ndugu.

'The locals, they're waiting for us to leave, so they can take over.'

'D'you think it will ever happen?'

He grinned. 'Yea. They'll chuck us out. And then they'll kill each other.'

'So what are you hanging on for?'

He shrugged. 'It's too beautiful to leave,' he said.

The tea came in translucent peach coloured cups. It was hot, deeply sweet and fragrant. Prem watched her take a sip. 'Sweet enough to knock your teeth out,' he said it for her.

Leila tried another sip. She recognised the taste of condensed milk.

'Hindi tea. We boil it all up together, tealeaves, water, milk. Just the job for shock, heatstroke, morning sickness. Anything like that'

A male scream came from the shed. The elder brother ran into the shop.

'Quick, bring tea.' Johnson had seen a snake under the Land Rover and was hysterical. His cries reminded Leila of her father - the sound of fear disguised as outrage. Shouting at a snake that had long since scuttled off and in any case had not touched him.

MUSCOVY DUCK CASSEROLE

1 Muscovy duck (about 2 kg)
50 g (2 oz) butter
2 peeled and slice onions
2 peeled and sliced carrots
2 garlic cloves crushed
a little plain flour
1 teaspoon tomato puree
175 ml water
275 ml red wine
1 teaspoon dried thyme
2 bay leaves
2 star anise
2 cinnamon sticks
zest and juice of two oranges

Joint the duck, or ask a butcher to do it for you. Heat the butter in a large casserole dish then season and brown the duck, a few pieces at a time and remove to a plate.

Add the onions, carrots and garlic to the fat and cook for about 10 minutes, stirring occasionally until the vegetables have turned golden brown. Add the flour and cook for a minute.

Pour in the water and wine and stir until the sauce boils, and then add the orange zest and juice, and the herbs and spices. Return the duck to the casserole dish, cover and cook in a preheated oven at 325F/ 170C/ Gas mark 5 for 1 ½ to 2 hours until the duck is tender.

Six months before her first child was due Leila received a letter from Ben with an astonishing item of news. The parents were together again living above a furniture shop in North London. Money left to their mother by the German aunt had done it.

By now Leila had given up her job with the agency and was freelancing. She sold a story to the San Francisco Chronicle about Elephant meat being used for canned dog food and made a killing with a story of a family sailing from Mombasa to New Zealand on a home made catamaran with the grandmother tethered on deck to her favourite chair. She had a regular agony column in a Sunday paper.

'I have been impregnated by my uncle,' an up-country schoolgirl wrote. 'I feel like a rotten mango,' an Asian girl confided, 'I have been deceiving my sister with her boy friend.'

Leila and Edmund were now living in a house shaped like a ship. Set in twenty acres of bush and fifteen miles from the city the single storey house had been designed by an ex sea captain. There were deck-like verandas on each side and a long sitting room in the centre. Two bedrooms at one end and a kitchen and larder at the other were fitted with porthole windows. There was a guesthouse and a garden with lawns with an ancient pepper tree and a plot for Chingili and Wambui to grow their maize and run a few hens.

'One of these days you must come out here,' Leila wrote to her brother and parents. 'You will be looked after like royalty.' Leila's mother sent a Woman's Own paper pattern for a baby's first gown with the note: 'Send me a ticket and I will come tomorrow. Your father is driving me nuts.'

Returning from the cinema one night Edmund slowed down for a body in the road. He was able just in time to accelerate and get away from a gang with pangas hiding in the bushes. This was a week after Len had been ambushed and attacked.

A radio station conducted a charity telephone auction for an orphanage. Edmund bid for two pairs of Muscovy ducks and made a pond for them. Within two months the Muscovies had multiplied to ten. Months later there were twenty-five.

'We'd better start eating them,' Edmund suggested.

For a reason they would not explain both Chingili and Wambui refused to slaughter the ducks. A neighbour sent his Kikuyu houseboy to do the job and Leila on waking from an afternoon nap looked out of the bedroom porthole to see the washing line hung with Muscovy corpses. Leila and Edmund gave a successful dinner party for twenty people. The dark rich gamy meat of the ducks was a talking point.

'We've solved it,' Edmund said. 'As soon as we're up to ten ducks again we'll throw another party.'

The Muscovies were not up to ten again in number when Edmund came home early one day. The glum news was that he had been Africanised. 'Time to push off,' he said.

PERFECT ENGLISH PORK CHOP

The best chops are from the chump end containing the fillet or from the rib end. Ask the butcher to cut the chops between 2 - 3 cm (¾ to 1¼ inch) thick. The backbone should be removed so that the chop can lie perfectly flat on either side. All but a thin layer of fat must be removed. Drink with a dry white wine or a rose.

For two people
2 pork chops
1 tablespoon lard for cooking oil
25 g (1 oz) butter
100 ml (¼ pint) dry white wine
Preheat the oven at 325F/ 163C/ Gas mark 5

Dry the pork chops. Heat the fat or oil in a casserole and brown the chops on either side for 3 minutes. Remove from heat.
Season with salt, pepper and some sage or thyme. Add butter, cover and heat until the meat is sizzling then place in the bottom of the oven for twenty five to thirty minutes, turning and basting when necessary. The chops are cooked when the juices show no sign of a pink colour when the meat is pierced.

Place the chops on a hot dish while you make a sauce.
Pour the wine into the casserole dish. Mix in with the liquid from the pork and the coagulated cooking juices. Boil rapidly to reduce and pour over the chops.

Currency restrictions made it illegal to transfer money out of the country. Edmund and Leila drove to the coast. 'Might as well blow the lot,' Edmund had decided 'before they take it off us.'

They booked into the most expensive room in the most expensive hotel. Leila was now heavily pregnant. The Rhodesian organiser of the wild life safari told Edmund he'd prefer not to take Leila along. 'Three Germans, two pairs of Americans and Japanese is going to be tough enough.' Edmund hinted at journalistic connections with travel page editors and the Rhodesian relented.

'You've got to promise me not to pup in the middle of the bush,' the Rhodesian joked, 'I can shoot, I can protect you from an elephant stampede, I can save you from a marauding lion. I can't deliver babies.'

They set off at dawn in two jeeps. The sky was streaked in aquamarine and gold. They came across giraffe and elephant and leopard, zebras and gazelles. They slept under canvas and were woken by the cries of wild dogs.

'Can't we stay in Africa?' Leila whispered. 'Just for a while longer.'

Edmund patted her swollen belly. 'Not with this.'

Edmund had no reason to return to England. His parents were in South Africa now. He had no desire to move south. 'It's a brutal place,' he said. 'You wouldn't like it.'

Like other Europeans they considered migrating to Australia, to New Zealand, to Canada, the safe countries. Australia sounded good to Edmund. He had good possibilities of a job there. Leila felt a kick inside her. 'Wait,' she addressed her belly. 'Wait till I'm ready.'

On their return to the hotel the management put on a magnificent feast by the swimming pool. The sound of the swishing sea made perfect music. A cliché full moon behind swaying palms lit the scene like a Hollywood set. At the far end of the swimming pool damask covered tables laden with dishes from East and West vied for attention. All the fruits of Africa and those imported from beyond were arranged tumbling from a giant shell - guavas, lychees, pineapples, breadfruit, kai apples, strawberries, apricots. On another table an entire kingfish glazed and decorated in aspic was the centre piece of a fruits of the deep display. Shellfish, octopus, flatfish and parrot fish were in attendance.

On the continental table there were chicken breasts, chicken legs, chicken in sauce, beef and lamb braised, roasted, grilled, olived, rolled, paprikared, curried, skewered. Vegetable dishes were in abundance mashed, fried, roasted sautéed, au natural and in sauces, stuffed and glazed, spiced herbed and curried. An array of salads on ice with and without dressing filled bowl and platters. Imported and local cooled beers, sundowners, wines and waters, sherries, brandies and whiskies arrived on demand.

Elaborations of meringue jostled with soufflés and sponges, jellies and moulded ices. A swan carved out of ice floated on pink water. A castle of a chocolate pudding dusted with sugar overlooked displays of biscuits.

Leila laughed to herself when Edmund returned with his plate of food to their table. On his plate was a pork chop, apple sauce, roast potatoes and peas and a glass of beer.

'What's that like?' she asked.

'Perfect', he smiled. 'What are you having?'

She swanned past the elaborate displays of food. 'Is there a herring?' Leila asked the Swedish chef.

'Herring is from cold waters,' he said. 'Try tilapia.' Tilapia often tasted muddy. 'What about a pickled herring,' she had a sudden desire for it.

'For that,' he said, 'you will have to go North, far away from the Equator.'

In the night she woke to tell Edmund she did not want to go to Australia. Not yet.

She wanted to return to England first.

'You're homesick, is that it?'

'Something like that.'

#####

Thank you for reading my book. If you enjoyed it please take a moment to leave a review at your favourite retailer.
Alex Adon

Thank you for trying my recipes, I hope you enjoyed them!
Caroline Krantz

"Tell, me what you eat and I will tell you who you are.'
(Jean Anthelme Brillat-Savarin 1755-1826)

About the author and the recipe devisor

Alex Adon is a prize-winning stage, film and television writer and an avid cook. This is her first published novel.

Caroline Krantz is a lifelong lover of food and cooking. Inspired by Middle Eastern and Eastern European roots and by her extensive travels, she regularly creates feasts for her family and friends. When not perfecting recipes or browsing food markets she writes English language teaching books that are used by students around the world.

Printed in Great Britain
by Amazon